One More River

ILLINOIS SHORT FICTION

One More River

Stories by
Lester Goldberg

UNIVERSITY OF ILLINOIS PRESS
Urbana   Chicago   London

"One More River," *Ascent,* vol. 1, no. 3, 1976
"The Sticking Room," *Epoch,* Spring, 1974
"The Reckoning," *National Jewish Monthly,* June, 1973
"Semper Fidelis," *Story Quarterly* 4, 1976
"The Witness," *National Jewish Monthly,* December, 1974
"The Cavalryman," *National Jewish Monthly*, December, 1973
"Sleeping," *Epoch,* Spring, 1975
"Joshua in the Rice Paddy," *Colorado Quarterly,* Spring, 1974

Library of Congress Cataloging in Publication Data

Goldberg, Lester, 1924-
  One more river.

  (Illinois short fiction)
  CONTENTS: One more river.—The sticking room.—
Decline and fall.—La causa. [etc.]
  I. Title.
PZ4.G619180n [PS3557.03578]   813'.5'4   77-9058
ISBA 0-252-00674-7
ISBN 0-252-00673-9 pbk.

For
Florence Bonime
and
Ethel Hepburn Paul

Contents

Contents

One More River

Just six months out of North Plainfield High School, in the winter of '32 when I hit the road.

Five dollars a week, my old man had promised me for working on the chicken farm. He and I shook hands on it. He never paid out a solitary dime and I saw how things were, just couldn't bring myself to ask him. My father came home from his cutter's job in the garment center in New York, and let's get a move on, he'd say, grab the tool box and we'll fix that fence post before supper.

He'd watch me for a minute, and when the saw bound in the four-by-four, he'd snatch it out of my hand, saying, call yourself a carpenter, you're a shoemaker. In the morning, he'd hammer on my door before six, and I was happier when he went off to work and I could take care of the moldy chickens without his advice.

Those few nights my father couldn't find any extra jobs around the chickens, I'd hustle over to the social center supported by the forty Jewish families in the rural area west of Plainfield; they called themselves the Settlers, mostly cloak and suit union men, one capmaker.

I belonged to the Jack London Cultural Club, fellows and girls from eighteen to twenty-four, three jobs among twenty of us. The club's literary contest, a tradition for four years, was almost scrapped that year because part of the group wanted to use the money to send a delegate to the Scottsboro trial.

The ten-dollar first prize went to the essay "The Scottsboro

Boys—A Lesson in Economic and Social Repression." But there was
a big fight in the club because the treasury was bare. The left-guard
activists had raided the treasury to send telegrams to the governor of
Alabama from different parts of the state of New Jersey—Newark,
Bayonne, Plainfield, Trenton, Atlantic City—all protesting the
Scottsboro conviction. I had enough hassling with my old man, and I
didn't take sides.

Just about that time, my father and the other chicken farmer–garment workers organized a cooperative to buy feed and eliminate the
middleman. They bought a carload of cornmeal. The first shipment
arrived in a railroad car in Bound Brook, forty tons to the car, one
hundred pounds to the bag, eight hundred bags. The feed was low-
priced: ninety cents a bag. Six volunteers helped unload the car and
then sprawled on the bags, guarding the shipment. Ziggy from last
year's football team and I wangled my father's truck and we got the
delivery job. My father would get gas and five dollars for the use of
the truck; Ziggy and me, two dollars apiece.

The chairman gave me seven dollars and the list of orders, then
went off to work. We lugged and unloaded from eight in the morning until nine o'clock that night. I dropped Ziggy off down the road,
then bone-tired I drove home and unloaded forty bags of feed into
our shed. Dark in there, and I didn't stack them the way my father
would want them stacked.

In the kitchen, I took off my boots, shoved them under the table,
and stretched my toes. Where's Pop? I asked my mother.

With the chickens, she said, where else. Rest, I'll get you a meat-
loaf sandwich.

My father came storming in, face like a red pepper. I counted
thirty-nine bags. Where the hell is number forty?

I didn't panic. I'll restack them in the morning, Pop.

Thirty-nine bags. I counted them. That's ninety cents, almost a
dollar wasted. Can you find ninety cents lying in the street?

He's standing right next to me now. I remembered the pushes and
shoves: my father's a pusher; when I didn't move fast enough, he
shoved me along. I started to get up. For chrissakes Pop, ninety
cents, I'll look—

He grabbed my shoulder, and smacked me across the face with his open left palm.

I'm up and swung on him, the first time, I swear it's the first time, and I looped my shot down so instead of the side of his jaw I've poked him in the chest. He swarmed over me, strong son-of-a-bitch, gurgling—hit your father, hit your father—his right hand at my throat, clawing at me with his left. I grabbed his right wrist with my right hand and chopped him on the chin with my left elbow, and I saw another pair of hands encircling his neck, my mother's hands yanking his chin back. I heard my mother screaming, stop it, stop it, you'll kill him, and he let go of my neck, and my mother's in between us, first shoving him on the chest, and when she shoved at me I just turned around and ran upstairs to my bedroom.

I closed the door and propped a chair under the knob. I threw myself on the bed, still in dirty work clothes. I couldn't sleep. I started repeating in my head four o'clock, four o'clock, and it worked because I awakened before my father, stole downstairs, got my shoes from under the kitchen table, and got out of his house. He welched on me, never paid me the five dollars a week; I hit him—had to—evens things a bit. My mother wouldn't miss me. She had my two younger brothers.

I walked past the chicken coops in pitch darkness; could hear the chickens messing around, maybe laying a couple of eggs, puffing up and squeezing the eggs out.

Tramp along until daylight when the iced-over puddles at the sides of the road start to crack and lucky to grab a ride on U.S. 1 into Philly. The first thing I do is go to the post office and buy a stamped envelope and mail my father the five dollars for the truck hire. I'm sorry I hit him but he had it coming. I still feel his fingers on my right cheek. Granted, he couldn't pay five dollars a week, but five dollars a month? Or every three months? A man needs real work, not chores. That leaves me with two dollars, my only payday in the last eight months. I cuss myself for a week for giving up the five dollars.

Now I'm getting freer and freer, so around the corner I buy six loose cigarettes, light one and put the others in my shirt pocket. A skinny kid with a curled-up used butt hanging from his lips asks for a light. I give him a fresh cigarette, and he lights up and puts the used one away. He sucks that smoke in, and a look comes over him like he's being invited into heaven.

Name's Willie Klinger, he says, walking alongside me. I keep walking but don't know where I'm walking to. I'm from Klingerstown, Pa., know where that is?

I shake my head no, in a friendly way.

Sunbury then. Same no shake from me.

My daddy's an undertaker, Willie talks on. I've been to mortician's school, learned how to paint them up, stuff cotton inside their jaws, make 'em look better than new. Nothing to undertake now, he says deadpan.

I grin, seeing as he expected me to.

Now my daddy says nobody's coming in, but the people hungry as they are must be dying even faster than before. My daddy says if we had a flood, and the Susquehanna overflowed, all those bodies buried in the backyards would just rise up and float down the road.

He paused, out of breath, not for long though. I'm backsliding Lutheran, he says. What are you?

Just living.

But what are you?

I was born Jewish but I don't hold with it. I'm called Miller.

I can see you don't know much, Willie says, so you better come along with me, and he turns right and I follow. How about another butt, he says, stretching out his hand.

After we eat, I'm starved.

You're one damn fool for not holding with the Jews. They give the best handouts, and I'd go with you, you just tell them we're both Jewish.

The hell with that!

The steam engine runs the West Virginia hills, hugging the mountainside, dragging the boxcars and open gondolas and black tankers along, running over the rickety trestles, the engine straining up the long grades, then charging down the hillside, the boxcar I'm in tip-

ping so the floor where I'm lying slants when you see the front of the
swaying trestle. I stretch out, the wheels clacking and squealing
under me, rest on one elbow and look through the partly open car
door, smoke rising from the hillside cuts and then a glimpse of a
cabin chimney. I see a mule pulling a Hoovercart, a sawed-off car
rear with a dog lying on the leather seat, a boy swatting the mule
with a branch, and I wouldn't mind being on the road and driving
along instead of freezing to death inside this coffin-dark freight,
while outside it's getting darker, a deep purple and ink-blotched
darkness and we hit the flat along the river and as we flow with it at a
steady pace I can see the silhouette of the train floating along upside
down, and I'm floating and I stick my head out the door aways,
hanging on to an iron car brace, and look for my head in the water
and then I see it riding upside down, and the engine slows and the
cars clank together and I hear one clank after another and the door
jars closed and I catch it with my hand before it cuts my head off.

It gets real quiet and the thirteen or so bums in the car sit there
not stirring and Willie gets up, I'll be right back, and he jumps
down. I watch him go into the bushes and squat down. A couple of
guys get up; water stop, one says; they jog around, swinging their
arms to get warm, when suddenly the train jerks forward and stops,
then starts again, and as it picks up speed, Willie bursts through the
bushes. So I shove the car door back and hang out, ready to give him
an arm up, but we're going faster. He sprints for the door, one arm
swinging, the other holding up his pants, and then he stops. I just
raise my hand and he raises his.

Now it's just me. On the car floor, Willie's blanket that he left behind, wrap it tight around me and close my eyes. The old man's
feeding chickens now. I loosen my belt and tuck in the newspapers
that Willie made me stuff around my back and sides. I move away
from the cutting wind coming through the door and take a last look
at the stars flying by. Close my eyes and open them. Someone's
coughing his guts out in the other end of the car. I close my eyes
again and hold them closed, drift off and then the rail shrieks along
my spine, the train halts and my head smacks against the wall. A
many-layered bum near the door shouts in a conductor's voice,

Richmond—Everybum Out—Last Stop.

Near the yard I find a dump of a coffee shop, and with my last coin I buy coffee and a stale roll for a nickel and get a dirty look when I ask for a phone book. I go out and walk around and the regular people are stirring, the ones who walk as if they got jobs to go to, easy to tell them from the bums who've just crept out of storefronts and move in no direction at all. I ask a guy in a veteran's cap, setting up his box of apples, for the way to the synagogue.

A stocky man in a long black coat is sweeping in front of the place. I wait while he finishes and then he goes to the high black iron gate and starts to open it.

I stand next to him and finally he has to look up at me. Can I work for a meal? I say.

I do the work, he says. That's all the work.

I'm Jewish sticks in my throat so I just stare at him.

The man says, go home!

I can't.

The rabbi is still asleep, he says. I wait. He pulls out a little notebook, looks in it, turns to a blank page, and holding the book against the synagogue sign on the fence, he talks as he writes. He digs in with his stubby pencil, go around the corner to Resnick's Restaurant, tell him, you shall love the stranger, and after you tell him, and after you eat, go to this address, and he gives me the note, then shoves me hard on the shoulder—another pusher, a Richmond pusher—Go!

What's gonna be, Miller? Miller, what's gonna be.

Miller, you're a bum!

Resnick, dirty white apron around his healthy belly, is frying eggs, six yellow bullseyes in butter and do they smell good and when I could get his attention, I deliver the message.

He wipes his forehead and looks at me hard. Rabbi Gershon again, eh, with his same cockamamie scriptures, go sit down there, you like eggs, yes, I see you like eggs, so sit on that stool, you smell better than Gershon's usual clientele.

That night I sleep free of charge in the attic of an old hotel, and just before I close my eyes, I remember my father never took charity and only one loan in his entire life, from the Jewish Agricultural Society, and this loan, his chickens and his sweat in the shop have almost paid back.

one more river to Jordan

Go on and going south now, and I hear, stay away from Flomington, Alabama, the railroad bulls will push you off a moving train, and I go through Greenville, an experienced bum now, where it's Schneider and Friedman, and they tell me Montgomery's a tough place but you can't avoid it, it's a rail center, but I get through and begin to forget the names, Lipschitz and Dolgow and in one place a guy called Merriweather but he was a Jew too. It's hot enough for anybody in Pensacola, Florida, and every place they tell me to go home, until I start saying that I'm an orphan so they'll leave me alone.

I eat raw shrimp from a can in back of a crazy Frenchman's truck in Gulfport, that's how hungry I am, and then in New Orleans I almost get caught for good. They stuff me with food and put me up with Chernetzsky, a housepainter, and he pays me wages and I sleep in his house. I've got the orphan story down pat, tell them I live with a cruel uncle on a farm, nothing to eat and the uncle won't let me go to school. After the second week I'm painting houses, all outside work, and Chernetzsky finds a niece for me and tells me I'm like a son to him and praises my work, but nags, nags, nags, at least call home.

A couple of days later, I cut out early in the morning. Ten dollars in my pocket and I'm heading for the Chicago World's Fair.

In the town of St. Louis, Missouri (really nowheresville), and I'm no country hick anymore. I've walked New York from the Battery to Spuyten Duyvil, and even Newark has Ruppert's Beer and the Newark Bears. I'm enjoying it all: Sally soup kitchen, Hallelujah, I'm a bum, Hallelujah, I'm a traveler, get moving from a cop and a shove with his nightstick when my feet dirtied the sidewalk in a good section of town, and twenty-five cents for taking out the slops in a greasy restaurant. I give a whole dime to go in to see *The Sign of the Cross*. Oh, the innocence of that milk-skinned Elissa Landi. The chariots go charging around the arena, and Frederick March gives the villain his comeuppance, not like real life—the Scottsboro Boys under death sentence again. At the end of the movie, March with a noble look on his face joins Elissa Landi and they both wait in the Roman arena to be served up to the lions.

Fox Movietone News. Jimmy Foxx cracks a home run. Then a cowboy-and-Indian cartoon flashes on. Three scouts are fleeing from a horde of howling Indians. One scout is dressed like Daniel Boone, coonskin cap and long rifle, but the other two are hunchbacked and have long noses, and their hats look like *shtreimels,* the black round hat you see on New York's Lower East Side. A stream of cussword symbols is pouring out of Boone's mouth and from the other two, I can hardly believe it—right to left, too, like my old primer—Jewish hieroglyphics appear on the screen. Boone is desperate, no more ammunition. He tells the two hook-nosed fellows: prepare to die bravely. They're holed up among a pile of rocks on a hillside. An Indian chief is climbing a cliff to attack them from the rear. One assistant says to the other: Herschel, give him a *zetz* in the *tsainer.* I can't make out Jewish anymore but can translate this into: Harry, give him a sock in the teeth. I laugh out loud. I roar. I howl. No one's joining in. Isn't it funny? Hilarious? My laugh's hollow now, can't stop; someone yells shut up and I know that in the entire theater not one person is laughing. Harry hits the Indian as directed and the other hunchback grabs the two pack mules, punches small holes in the huge packs, and sends the mules off at a gallop. The trade goods fall out and all the Indians chase after it, stopping to pick up pieces as the stuff falls. Boone, Harry, and the assistant hop on Boone's horse and the three escape. When the lights go on, I just sit there, can't make myself get up; fellows and girls walk out holding hands, and fathers herd smaller kids up the aisles. Guess they forgot hard times for a couple of hours.

one more river

I'm heading north: what's gonna be, Miller? Miller, what's gonna be! Don't seem to see the scenery anymore, don't know anyone, there's hot places and cold places and trees and railroad yards and more cops pushing and the Jewish Centers, the Young Men's Hebrew, and they're all saying, go home, go home and it all looks the same.

I'm sitting in a car with a bunch of hobos, like the last bunch, just more Negroes down here, and the 'bos seem younger, almost kids some of them, fifteen or sixteen, when it hits me—I'll go to Decatur —thousands of miles ago sat it out in Jersey while my friends screamed—screw literature—send a witness—I read in the paper that the Scottsboro trial had been moved to Decatur after the first conviction was reversed, and Sam Leibowitz of New York was on his way to meet the other attorneys and organize a defense. The trial was on now in late March.

When I hit Decatur, I'm pretty stubbly-faced to attend a trial with a bunch of strangers. A nice-looking town, reminds me of my home-town, Plainfield, with its broad tree-lined streets, branches arching over and meeting overhead so the country follows you right into town. Lots of good large homes with big porches on the front and fine lawns. The town's boiling up for so early in the morning, wagons filled with overalled farmers going by and carloads of men all going in the same direction. Shotguns and deer rifles are lying in the back seats of a couple of cars. I drift along and take off my jacket and then my sweater, roll up the sleeves of my blue-striped shirt, the shirt's cleaner than the sweater, and hope I'll pass muster. Reach the Decatur courthouse, a white brick building with those big Confed-erate white columns out front and a large oak tree at the side en-trance with four National Guardsmen standing in front of the tree. They're carrying rifles, and an old farmer walking by points to the tree and calls out, there's the hangin' tree.

I get on the line for whites and as we approach the door, two town marshals begin frisking everyone. Why'd you bring that handgun, I hear one big marshal say to a guy wearing a black suit jacket over blue overalls. Just bein' prepared, the man answers. The marshal gives him the thumb and he cusses his way down the courthouse steps.

Finally I'm inside, one of the last to make it. I sit down third seat from the door. The fans are lazily spinning overhead and all the south windows in back of me are covered by dark shades, but it's hot as blazes and smells like a barnyard. There's a small Negro section off to my right. The Negro men are very quiet and stare straight ahead. Almost everyone's in shirtsleeves; some farmers in overalls, teeth brown-stained from chewing tobacco, a few better-dressed people in shirts and bow ties, carrying straw hats.

The nine Scottsboro Boys are sitting up front and they're not handsome. Patterson, the tallest, looks like a good guy to avoid if he hopped into your boxcar; but I'd swear there are two little fellows no older than my brother; they couldn't be more than thirteen or fourteen. Those kids, rape someone? There's Leibowitz. He's listening as carefully to Patterson as if that ugly mug is his son. I want to wave to him. He looks cool for a big guy, beginning to put on weight. Good old Leibowitz: the heavyweight champion of defense lawyers. Wonder if he'd take my case: defend a man who's accused of stealing a ninety-cent bag of chicken feed. In back of me I hear, be a miracle if he leaves town alive. Then in front, one young farmer is telling another about a baseball game, the first of the season: that goddamn referee was a Hartselle man, weren't one of ourn, he Leibowitzed us right out of the game. Fellow next to me says, where you from, son? I look at him, don't like the twist to his mouth. Answer, Georgia, I'm from Georguh.

He gets up then, a stringbean of a fellow; he's wearing a seersucker jacket, and as he walks away his jacket opens, and I swear I see a handgun in a holster at his side. This lawman walks down the center of the aisle and standing next to the judge is a hefty gent with an even bigger gun tied down, and the skinny fellow, without turning his head, is talking and his chin is wagging in my direction, and the fat fellow is nodding his head.

I'm up, slide fast over the two fellows between me and the aisle, almost step into the gold spittoon on my way out, and I scoot down those steps. Force myself to slow down: the place is ringed with Guardsmen in leggings commanded by a Guard officer in polished brown boots. I look back but don't see anyone following and I walk faster, heading toward the railroad station.

I hide in a culvert near the station until dark. It turns colder when the sun goes down so I decide to pop into the men's room and warm up, then grab the first freight going north. I stay in the bathroom about a half-hour, and figure better not press my luck so I swing the

door open and step out. Slide right back in. They're out there, three
of them, and I wonder if they've seen me. I chin myself up to the
screen-covered window at the side of the john and spy the skinny
marshal and two others with him, swinging clubs. They're moving
very slowly but they're ambling toward the john. Certain they'll peer
in. Worse if they catch me inside, with the station deserted; more
'bos must be waiting somewhere for the night freight but not around
here. I walk out the door trying to appear unconcerned. Drifting,
they're drifting toward me, closing the circle, the thin man in the
middle and the other two swinging wide to either side. I turn right,
walking toward one club, and still the skinny guy is closing in,
doesn't say anything but he's opened his jacket and his thumb
latches onto his belt. I'm up to the man with the club, just a second
fella, he says, and I bolt for it, dash to the left and cut back, and run
like hell down the entire length of the platform, certain a bullet will
slam into my back. No one yells and I can't look back. I head for a
small shack at the end of the platform; if I can duck around it, the
shack's between me and the guns. I slip on the gravel, hear two shots
in quick succession, puff of dust off to my side, and I roll aways and
spring to my feet, dodge behind the shack, keep running, cut into
the woods, come to a narrow stream, leap across it, keep running,
smack my head on a branch, crash through a thicket, can't go much
farther, and I stop for a second to listen for the hounds, can't hear
any hounds, easy now, Miller, easy Miller—can't hear anything except my own heavy panting, the moon's out, a half-moon, but I'm
seeing double up there, two half-moons. I hear the night-train
whistle. Missed it.

Spend the night shivering in a thicket like a hunted rabbit, and in
the morning I work my way deeper into the woods; later drink from
a cold brook and eat two hard biscuits, left over from yesterday's
breakfast. Afraid to forage for food, I skulk in the woods the rest of
the day. Toward evening, guiding myself by the sound of the train
whistles, I begin to work my way out of the woods. I'm afraid to go
into the station so I wait just outside, figuring I'll get on the middle
of a long, slow one, hop on as it's pulling out but hasn't picked up
speed. I'm hungry enough to eat my belt. I poke deep into my

pockets and pick out a few biscuit crumbs and suck them off my fingers.

I let SOUTHERN SERVES THE SOUTH roll by, every last faded red, cracker-barrel boxcar, and wait for anything else. Now one's headed in the right direction—NORTH—and I let leventeen or so cars go by and then burst out of the woods and head for an open door and scramble aboard. Four-five hobos stretched out in the back. The train pokes along through a small dark woods, then an overgrown field with a bony white horse foraging in the moonlight; up a slight grade now, and as the train slows down—first one, then another, then a third black guy appears draped over the car door ledge.

Next car, next car, I hear someone holler from the shadows. The three Negroes perch half in the car, elbows and hands on the car floor and bodies hanging out. An overalled guy, detaching himself from the darkness, moves toward the Negroes with a shuffling, dancing step. He's a tall blond-haired kid, and he's prancing in front of the three Negroes. He's wearing torn black high sneakers; moving forward, then back, motioning toward the three with his palms as if he's scattering chicken feed. Suddenly, one hand shoots out and stiff-arms the Negro nearest him on the shoulder and the boy slides back and drops off. The other two still hang there. The blond kid dances toward them, in a fighter's crouch, shooting lefts and rights into the air.

What's gonna be, Miller?

Miller—what's gonna be!

The train is picking up speed. The utility poles flash by. Murder, to push them off now.

End of the line, Miller. On your feet, Miller!

I stand up at last. I sway, can't focus on him. A lean boy in the usual overalls. Little taller than me, not as heavy.

Lay off, I tell him. We don't do that. He turns. I face him, the open door to my left; afraid to stand between him and the guys hanging onto the lip of the door. I fix on his left overall buckle, broken, a safety pin's holding it together. The train's clipping along. My hands hang loose. I don't bring them up, don't want to force his hand, give him his pride. I lock his eyes, the color of washed-out jeans. To do any finger-stomping now, he's got to turn his back on me—I'd grab his overalls and take him down from behind. He turns away and slouches to the back of the car. The two Negro boys get on and go to the other end. I sit down in the middle. No one says one word. I'm light-headed again and starving.

one more river to cross

Over one hundred years ago, before there was a Depression, my father took me to New York to the old neighborhood to show me where he used to live on the East Side and to break me into the egg business. We'd had the farm only two years then, I'd just turned thirteen.

We finished carrying the eggs into the market and were leaning against the fender of Pop's truck. My father had just bought me a bag of hot chestnuts, so hot I could hardly hold the bag in my hand. I kept juggling the bag from one hand to the other. A sturdy old woman, carrying a rope-tied, large black valise, walked up to my father. She dropped the valise at his feet, and pulling her shoulders back, she stood erect. Take me to Long Island, she said, in Yiddish.

He stared her down. What do I look like, a taxi driver?

The woman said, I need you to take me.

Get in, my father said to her. To me he said, she's crazy. Doesn't she see my Jersey license? Son, help her with the valise. He shoved me so I'd move faster but it wasn't a hard shove.

The car floor is cold and hard. I sit cross-legged, rocking forward and back to the rhythm of the wheels. I turn my face toward home.

The Sticking Room

The third time Arnie Weingarten returned to the Commons, that gray gothic pile with high slit windows, he admitted to himself: he must find out if Goldalee was a girl, not a woman as he first imagined.

Last night, she had started a whole chocolate cake for him, cutting a huge wedge in it, and smiled at him in a special way. This girl-woman, almost six feet tall, filled his tray with more mashed potatoes and vegetables for sixty cents than he had ever received at Ida Noyes's house or the Co-Op. When she turned away, and waved her ladle at another girl saying, get some more mash, the cowboy's back, he quickly examined her backside. He knew her long straight nose and full cheeks with two deep dimples. Her breasts were large, but maternal. No thrust to them. If they didn't actually sag, they were still too low on her chest. The behind was squarish and looked strongly girdled without the bouncing promise of a young girl's. Her legs, he quickly decided, eyes traveling downward, were utilitarian, not heavy just not contoured, made to carry a large person from place to place.

She turned back to him while he hesitated over the dessert counter and if he wanted apple pie, it was too late. Are you really from Texas, she said, looking into his eyes; then when he looked down she had already deposited a slab of chocolate cake on his tray. Wal, I guess I am, ma'am. Dallas. Dallas, Texas. He took his tray to an empty table in a far corner, wondering how a street in South Dallas with a streetcar running day and night and helping behind the counter in his father's Army and Navy store made him a Texan.

He ate quickly, stoking himself, scanning the headlines in the *Sun-Times,* strange island names: Bongao, Sanga Sanga, Tawitawi, and Sammy, lighter than air, Sammy's out there. When he looked for her behind the counter, he noted she had the same big grin for everyone. And he knew, his brother Sammy, the chocolate cake gummed in his mouth, his brother Sammy would never give a girl like this—a second glance.

Sammy the valedictorian, Sammy the cross-country runner, Sammy the graceful dancer. Slim dark good-looking Sammy whom every Jewish mother in Dallas wanted for her daughter. Yet he was modest and kind to Arnie, and Arnie felt disloyal when he thought, a Jewish Andy Hardy.

Once he did something UnSammyish. Dad wouldn't let him have the car and he refused to go on a date without it. He called the girl and said he was sick. A half-hour later, this winner in the Queen Esther contest came over to keep Sammy company. He had just enough time to run upstairs, get into bed, and pull the covers up to his chin. Arnie let the girl in and tiptoed upstairs in front of her and told her she could only stay a short time because it might be catching. When she left, Sammy invited Arnie into his bed and told him the story of Davy Crockett and how Davy returned to the Alamo to help Jim Bowie and the other Texans. And the Jews too? Arnie asked. No, just the Texicans, Sammy said, who were fighting the Mexicans, and Davy and Jim were the only two left alive and Davy clubbed three Mexicans defending Jim, and Jim threw his knife from his sickbed defending Davy and then they were both bayoneted. Sammy stayed home Monday too, and Arnie was surprised that his mother didn't holler and call him a loafer which he was. Just this once.

What are you staring at? she said. Mind if I sit down? She's down and he pulled his size thirteen brown wing-tipped shoes under the table, rocking it so her coffee sloshed into the saucer, no boots for him like those Dallas drugstore cowboys. He saw a little bead of sweat on her upper lip and she smelled strongly of some kind of toilet water and woman smell. Pink strong upper arms. Brown trusting heifer's eyes that made him turn away and he pointed to the news-photo in the *Sun-Times*—three men struggling to raise the American flag on Iwo Jima.

Arnie tapped the flag with his finger. How would you feel about a brother like this? My brother Sammy's out there somewhere, and Sammy's tailing a Jap fighter and Sammy is squeezing the triggers on both machine guns, badabababang bang, badabababang bang, and now a Kamikaze Jap is on Sammy's tail and he climbs and climbs into the clouds and the Jap climbs after him, and Sammy climbs higher—Easy now, Tex, she said, and put her hand over his wrist. Tell me about Texas. Ever see the Alamo?

I'd never go near it. Never been in San Antone. They can shove their cowboys and longhorns and fat-tailed Texas Rangers. Just shove'em. I left all that junk behind. I'm here to learn, learn everything there is to know. Drop Dallas into Chicago and you couldn't find it.

Get me some apple pie, she said, and vanilla ice cream. And more coffee. Tell the girl in the red blouse it's for me, you won't have to pay. He rose obediently. She said, did you make a face when I asked for ice cream too? No I didn't. I thought you looked disapproving, she said. No, he said. Eat what you want. Are implying I'm too heavy? she said. No, not at all. Not one bit. You carry your weight. I mean you carry yourself well. I like tall girls. I weigh one hundred and sixty-five, she said. I weigh two hundred and thirty-five, he said. Yeah, she breathed, from someplace deep down in her diaphragm, yeah; not the ye-ahhh of his coach who said ye-ahhh, you ought to lose twenty pounds, but yeah that sounded like yay or hip hip hooray.

Goldalee joined him for dessert every night, and on her first night off he took her to see *La Grande Illusion.* He became the French aviator Jean Gabin, cosily living on a German farm with Goldalee while the war stood still (a few in the audience booed and hissed when Von Stroheim or other Germans turned up), and when duty called Gabin back to France and Goldalee shaded her eyes to watch him leave across the snow-covered valley, Arnie's eyes were moist and he hid it from her, he hid it. She asked his age and he said, defiantly, eighteen, and she announced in a precise way, I'm exactly twenty-nine months older than you are. And he wondered if some pledge had been made with that mutual confidence.

When Arnie met Goldalee's father, she introduced him as the man she might marry someday. The little father craned his neck to look up at the son-in-law and Arnie expected a joking response, and it didn't come and Arnie knew he'd best step carefully because Goldalee said exactly what she meant at all times.

There was Benjamin, a sixteen-year-old thin Polish refugee that Arnie knew had been with the family for eight years, and nine-year-old Selena who was the family pet and insisted on measuring Arnie while Goldalee prepared dinner. Selena measured Arnie in her bedroom where the door jamb was marked off in feet and then took a yardstick and raised it above the six-feet mark, and ran into the living room to shout that Arnie was six feet five inches tall, the biggest man she had ever measured, and Arnie held his arm out straight and Selena chinned on it; then they all sat down and asked questions and Arnie showed Sammy's picture in his air force uniform, and they praised Sammy and Benjie cracked his knuckles and watched Goldalee and asked about football at S.M.U. and why didn't Arnie go to that football school, and Arnie called it a dopey game for musclebound idiots and Benjie's Adam's apple gulped and he watched Goldalee as she crossed the kitchen to go into the dining room and set the table, and the father said that before his wife died they had moved to this house so Goldalee would be close to the university and she could walk to school and the dinner was superb but Arnie felt them all watching him eat and took smaller helpings and only one piece of chocolate cake, and he was still hungry when he wandered into the kitchen where Goldalee was washing the dishes and offered to help. He thought about her warm, wonderful family and how they made him feel at home, the first home he had been invited to since he arrived in Chicago a year ago, and Goldalee washed and he dried in silence and he heard her father call from the living room—Goldalee, Goldalee, and a third time while she continued washing, Goldalee-lee-lee-lee-lee, lee-lee-leely, and Goldalee said to

Arnie, her wet soapy hand on his elbow, I've got to get out of here.

In the next few weeks, Arnie had little time for Parrington although he carried it under his arm to Goldalee's and they tried to wait for the family to get to bed but Benjie always hung around watching and asking questions and Arnie never knew when he'd come downstairs for a drink of juice or stick his head into the living room to ask a stupid question.

She invited him to lunch one Saturday, casually mentioning that the family would be away visiting relatives, and he came to the door and she opened it, wearing a yellow terrycloth bathrobe just above the knees, her brown hair still stringy from her bath and soap-smelling clean and she took his arm and they went right to the living-room couch where they had sat close together and upright for so many evenings and he knew this would be the one big moment in his life, and their arms were around one another in a jiffy and he found his hand under the robe clutching the fullness and softness of her and unable to contain it, even in his large hand, as it overflowed him and suffused him, and what did Sammy do the first time, and she drew him down and he found himself warm and warmer and her hand boldly was inside his waistband, stroking his belly, and he wished he had read a book or two so he would know what to do or listened to his friends more closely, and he lay alongside her and he was on fire, caught fire, fire, fire, fire, fire, he sobbed with it, and as he turned into her he clutched her shoulders and there didn't seem to be enough room for them, his knee, the right one, bumped against the side of the couch, he heard a hard knock on the door, and she said, don't mind it—and another louder knock and he rolled back, listening, and she slid out from under him and refastened the yellow robe and went away into the long hall. While he heard her voice murmuring from far away, he cooled, he subsided, he despaired and again began to rack his brain for everything he knew, everything he had heard, for some clues, and when she pattered back he felt despairing. He was approaching the most sublime test of his entire life and he knew nothing. Nothing.

She took his hand and said, let's go into the sunroom, adding reassuringly, the couch there has no back. We'll be more comfortable.

They hugged standing up before the couch, straining against one another and then tumbled down on it, no preliminaries—he saw her lick her lips and she reached for him, he felt cold, and turned heavily on her, hopefully stretching his eyes wide to look at the rosy skin, hoping and sinking on her, but still he felt cold and drawn. It's no use, he said, as she cradled his head on her bosom, it's no use. She reached for him once more, began to fondle him as he grew hopeful and wary, but hopeful, and then she said, I must cut up the salad. Let me up, Arnold dearest.

He got up and lumbered into the kitchen after her to sit heavily on a chair while she took out tomatoes and lettuce and cucumbers. Arnold, she said, while she arranged the offering in a wooden bowl. Arnold, there's plenty of time, Arnold. A lassitude overcame him. His limbs were outstretched, floating, all of him floating in a lukewarm bath. There seemed, indeed, to be plenty of time. All the time he would ever need. He floated.

Arnie left Goldalee's before the watchful Benjie and the others returned and when he arrived at his rooming house, his landlady handed him the telegram. Come right home. Sammy took sick. Urgent. Dad.

His room had a broken door lock so he packed everything into one large suitcase and two barracks bags that had been a gift from Sammy. Closet, drawers, and bookshelves cleared, he staggered out the door, pinning a note on it for Goldalee, and dragged the stuff down the stairs. Two trips. Bus on corner of Fifty-fifth Street and drag everything aboard. Two trips. The driver cursed his slowness. Couple of army p.f.c.s. jeered, can't take all that junk to camp. The dark blue Worumbo overcoat his father had bought him a year ago against the Chicago winds weighed heavily; he's carrying an anvil on each shoulder. Off at the Illinois Central Electric. Carry suitcase and one bag and then return for the other bag. Get a seat and stow the bags, takes several times two trips. Along the Lake Shore, they said the lake is beautiful, the soldiers have pretty girls seated with them —what could be the matter with Sammy? To old Lasalle Station— four trips, the air force guys in pink dress uniform have even more beautiful girls than the soldiers— to Kansas City—four trips—to

Dallas. His coach at Forest High School had said: your upper trunk is strong enough, use your weight—you can stop anyone—work on the footwork—jump through tires—jump through tires—jump through tires.

Arnie dropped his bags in his room and he and his father grabbed a cab to the hospital. Sammy, on leave, had complained of splitting headaches. He had been rushed to the hospital. Something pressing on the brain. The doctors explored. The doctors hacked out a tumor. His mother sat hunched up and staring at her shoes. She didn't look at Arnie even when he kissed her. Arnie went in alone. Behind the screen lay Sammy, white and drawn, his head swathed in bandages. How's football, Sammy said. Arnie sat straight in the white metal chair. He almost replied, no football at Chicago, you know that. Then he played the brother's game. Fine, fine, he said. I got into one game this week. We only lost 48 to 0. Wonderful, Sammy whispered, and last week? Much worse, Arnie said. I didn't play. We lost 68 to 0. They needed you, Sammy said.

Sammy crooked his finger. Arnie bent over him, his ear close to Sammy's mouth. Good sweet Sammy's breath stank. Sammy said so low Arnie strained to hear, the eagles they fly high—the fucking Jewish eagles—take the ring. Off my finger and hold it for me, Arnie boy. Arnie took the silver snake ring. Sammy used to call it his lucky ring. Arnie went out and turned at the door to give the V for Victory sign.

What did you talk about? Is he any better? Arnie's father said. Nothing, Arnie answered. He gave me this ring.

Sammy died three days later.

Arnie wandered into Sammy's still bedroom. Everything in place. The Navajo throw rug drawn tight over the bed. Arnie fingered Sammy's ties. His father walked in: don't touch anything. Arnie dropped the tie. Arnie's father said, matter-of-factly or maybe curiously, why don't you cry. Arnie walked out.

In the bathroom, he tried to cry. *I'm glad he's dead.* He pushed this thought down. He tried to cry. It came up. He pushed it away. He didn't cry. It crept on tiny rat's feet around and around his skull. He struck his left ear with the flat of his hand. A hard blow. To drive it out. It came out of his right ear. It came back through his left ear even though he held one hand over it, closing it. He thought blank. He willed blank. It came back. He dropped Sammy's ring into the toilet and flushed. The ring refused to go down and lay in the still water. Arnie flushed the toilet again.

Arnie asked his father if perhaps Mom would feel better if he didn't go back to Chicago. He could transfer to S.M.U. Only a mile walk to school.

No! Your mother won't feel better. Go back to school. Harshly his father said this. Softly, softly his father said, she'll get over it.

Arnie said to himself: *I'm repacking in a peculiar way. I'm peculiar.* Things he needed in the suitcase; other things he'd carry in the barracks bags. Books go into the barracks bags. He rescued Parrington. Into the suitcase with P.

Arnie fled back to Chicago. No need to return to his former empty room. He checked the valise and two useless barracks bags in Union Station, bought a ticket for New York—one way—and then he waited for the banks to open. Drew out his remaining savings and then returned to Union Station, reclaimed only the suitcase and boarded the train for New York.

In Manhattan, he walked down Forty-second Street from Grand Central Station. He stopped counting at fifteen movie houses, after he had already counted: seven cowboy pictures, five war films, three gangster films, five tit pictures, and a French movie at the Apollo. He paid nine dollars, one week's rent in advance, for a room on Twenty-eighth Street near Ninth Avenue. He thought he was lucky the next day when he found a job bussing and washing dishes in a diner on Tenth Avenue. While he gathered and stacked and filled the dish-washing machine and closed it and opened it, the steam pouring out, he did not think about Sammy. About anyone.

A whey-faced man put his hand on Arnie's right knee in the Apollo while he was watching *The Baker's Wife* and Arnie froze for a moment until the man's hand and little mice fingers walked along his thigh toward his crotch. He ran out while Raimu cried on the screen. The following day he bumped his head twice on the kitchen door frame, forgetting to stoop when he returned with a load of dishes. Then he picked up a saucer and coffee cup and the patron wasn't finished and grabbed the other end of the saucer, he'd have put it back if the man had only said something, but the cup tipped into the man's lap. The owner said Arnie was a nice fella and gave him two days' pay, but too big for this line of work.

On Eleventh Avenue and Fortieth Street he started his new career. The Boss openly admired his Six Feet Five frame and believed him when he said he was twenty years old. The swarthy Albanian who broke him in called himself Mumtaz. He said his mother named him Mumtaz, an East Indian name, because she liked the sound of it. Call me Mummy, he told Arnie, and I don't believe you're a Texan. You're big enough but you got no boots, your ears too big, and you too dark. Talk Texan, he commanded. Arnie dredged up a high school song and sang in a monotone: God Bless You Texas/And Keep You Brave and Strong/That You May Grow in Power and Worth/Throughout the Ages Long. The song satisfied Mummy and he gave Arnie a long-handled iron rake and Arnie followed him out of the locker room. Mummy said, you'll need different shoes, high ones but never mind now, we'll get you some after work.

The pigs were in fifteen or twenty pens all around the outer perimeter of the red brick building. Arnie tried to stop breathing. The stench like four and twenty stopped-up and overflowing outhouses, with a hundred-pound pig (Mummy told him these weren't full-grown porkers) sitting on each seat. Each pig had diarrhea and was shitting the close-packed fetid shit of Jews jammed together in a railway car and bound for—Arnie forced himself to believe. At one end of the huge, many-penned room, a spiral wooden ramp started from the concrete floor and circled dizzyingly up two floors. The second floor also had pens for pigs, cantilevered out above the concrete ground floor. Arnie saw high up, at the end of the ramp, a wooden green door. I'm opening the first pen, Mummy said, stand there and drive 'em up the ramp to the sticking room. Mummy opened the pen and thirty or so pigs jammed together came pouring through the narrow gate and Arnie headed them toward the ramp. Good pigs all, they climbed, stepping nimbly over the rough cleats on the ramp, shitting and pissing on the way up. Mummy clambered up behind them, nudging a straggler here and there with his rake while Arnie waited below. Then they emptied a second pen, and Mummy went inside to stir up a reluctant pig, saying to Arnie, you drive 'em up now, Tex. Arnie went up behind these pigs, heard Mummy yelling Ki-Yi-Yippy/Yippy Yay/Yippy Yay, and he slipped in their slime, almost falling when a pig tripped and came rolling down stopped by his knees, cuddling up to Arnie, then the pig got up to rejoin the others. The sticking-room door opened and Arnie saw two giant black men, stripped to the waist, working inside.

The pigs cried as soon as they entered the room. They all hollered, I want my momma, I want my momma, I want my momma. Arnie held the door open a crack to watch. No one would believe him. Not Sammy if he were alive, not Goldalee, not anyone. The two men grabbed a pig, wrestled the pig on its side, and fastened a chain to its left leg; then the motor started and the pig swung on a pulley that traveled across the open far side of the sticking room, and the pig swung on its left leg, hanging head down, snout and quivering belly facing the sticking room. The other milling pigs screamed. Another pig was grabbed, always the left hind leg, leg tied and sent after his friend. And another. And finally the cuddly pig and Arnie slammed the door. Arnie couldn't breathe. He forgot the stink while a giant hand squeezed his heart and lungs. And squeezed harder. He heard Mummy yelling at him to come on down. Looking to his right, he saw the pigs all swinging along, facing him until they reached a platform halfway down the building, a platform that formed an extension from the catwalk and ran under the pulley, and on the platform stood a small man wearing glasses, an array of gleaming knives to his right. He cut the pigs' throats with one deft motion, reaching up and stretching a bit as they came swinging along; the man stretched because he was a rather small man. When the pulley stopped and the last twitching pig, blood dripping from its throat, passed by his platform, the man, just an ordinary man, pulled a rag from his back pocket and wiped the blood from his glasses and then wiped the knife with the same rag and dropped the bloody flag over the platform and it floated down, down to the floor below.

Arnie slipped and slithered down the ramp and at the turn a

passel of pigs swept up toward him, one of them struck against him and he almost fell. The pig leaned against him for a moment, loving him, and then pissed on his foot. Arnie lashed out with the pointed toe of his wingtips. I'm sorry, pig, he whispered as the pig continued up the ramp and disappeared through the green door.

While he was eating his lunch in the diner down the avenue, a broad-chested black man got off his stool and said to his white-undershirted friend, that boy smell worse than niggers. Arnie stared down at his tuna-fish sandwich. Naw, the other man said, he smell worse than white man say Negroes smell. That's a real bad-smellin' boy. The owner came over and stopped in front of Arnie. Son, he said in a soft voice, you're from the slaughterhouse. We get the same trouble whenever they get a new man. You can eat at that corner table today but change your clothes before you come in again. Arnie's eyes watered at the kindness and he picked up his sandwich, milk, and chocolate cake and took them to the far corner, where he sat down before an open window.

That evening he wrote to his father and then to Goldalee.

Dear Goldalee:

I am working hard in a pig slaughterhouse and it really opens one's eyes. What an exhilarating experience! I talk to Negro truck drivers and prostitutes and swarthy Albanians.

I expect to visit the New York Public Library soon and continue my studies on my own. I might go up to the top of the Empire State Building or out to the Statue of Liberty even though they're for tourists not working people. I am not *at all* lonely. I'm feeling very fit.

Yours,
As ever—Arnie.

P.S. Why Sammy and not someone else?

P.P.S. I didn't have time to call when I got back from Texas. Did you get the note I pinned on my door before I left?

At the end of the week Mummy said to him, the Boss likes you. He told me he never seen the shit fly from those pens so fast. You're lucky. You got a job for life!

With his pay, Arnie bought a pair of steel-tipped work shoes, two blue chambray shirts, and a pair of moccasins. He threw out the brown wingtips because even after several airings on the window sill, the odor never left them.

The second week passed like the first. The fourth week brought an unusually sickly lot of pigs. Each morning he smelled the sweetish stench and he knew that another dying pig had been chewed up by rats the night before. After Mummy ran the healthy pigs up the ramp, Arnie would hammer on the gate of the pen, and approach the fallen pig gingerly where it lay on its side, its belly gnawed open, the entrails pouring out of it, slimy and dirty white and yellow and glistening. Always he tapped first, in case a rat was still gorging. Now he was more afraid of the short-legged waddling rats, the fattest and biggest ones he'd ever seen, fatter than prairie dogs, than anything in the entire city of New York.

A few hazy days went by and on Friday, payday, he was hosing down a pen, constricting the stream from the nozzle with his fingers and accentuating the force of the water, making a game of it to avoid scraping the dried shit loose with the rake, when he experienced a REVELATION.

He no longer cared about Sammy, no longer minded the pig sticking, and then began while awake and half-awake and asleep—THE ANOINTING.

He anointed Goldalee's long outstretched body as she lay on her belly naked, he anointed her shoulders and rubbed them and kneaded her back, rubbing her gently with a pale saffron-colored sweet-smelling soft oil, and anointed and kneaded her full hips, and further down too. And once he tickled the soles of her feet she trusted him completely, and she laughed a beautiful clear laugh. And he knew what to do; always now, he knew what to do.

In the Roman arenas in the olden days, occasionally when a fallen gladiator lay on the hot sand, lay there stoically, if the crowd shouted its approval loudly enough, and if the Roman emperor in the royal box had supped and wined well the night before, and if he had no indigestion on that morning, and if he was sufficiently cooled by the fans of the Nubian slaves, why then he just might gesture with his thumb up and the fallen gladiator would be permitted to live. It happened rarely.

Here if he wheeled a struggling sick pig to the gray-hatted U.S. Dept. of Agriculture man who sat in the small office, hat tipped back and reading the racing form—it was always thumbs down. Paradoxically the USDA man would thumb up, too tired to talk, but the thumb in one direction meant: wheel the pig to the sticking room; in the other direction: to the trash bin.

Somehow, on Sunday night while he sat in the low worn green armchair in his room, smoking a cigarette, the hurried surge of footsteps and the peremptory knock on the door came as no surprise. Arnie, Arnie, open the door. Goldalee opened it and walked in, a Marshall Field's shopping bag in her left hand and several paper bags cradled in her right. She flew toward him, crying Arnie, and he raised his right foot so that his bare right sole came up, almost against her charging midriff. He stubbed the cigarette in the ashtray.

She turned aside, ignoring the foot, and placed a cake box next to Parrington on the white enamel table and unhurriedly took two quarts of milk from the brown bag and placed them next to the box. Still she did not turn back to him, and she repositioned the milk and the cake box away from the table edge and fussed with them as if she were arranging flowers in a vase. Now she turned to Arnie. He sat both feet flat on the floor, his hands grasping the chair arms. How did you find me?

You're cruel, Arnie. You really are. You wrote to me and didn't give me your address. So I wrote your father. Got your Dallas address from the registrar. Your father wrote back that you threatened to cross the ocean—go even farther away—if he came to New York and tried to get you to come back home. You didn't answer his letters. She waited. Come home, Arnie! We all miss you. Selena and Benjie and Pop, and especially me. You sure stink!

Arnie said, there is a great deal to be learned here. Upton Sinclair's book *The Jungle* takes on new meaning. I regard this as one of the most important experiences of my life—to see the other side—

and furthermore—

You like it! Killing pigs!

I don't actually kill them. I just—

You're gentle with them, Arnie?

Well, no, but I have to take the lame ones and—

And what, Arnie?

I grab their ears—

Does it hurt, Arnie?

I grab their ears and hoist them on a dolly and take them to the USDA man—

Do it gently, do you Arnie?

No! They try to bite.

Arnie, why are you punishing yourself?

I'M NOT. It's a great experience. It's all part of life. You eat meat. Everyone eats meat and now I know, now I know, I know—

Goldalee pulled a coonskin cap from the shopping bag and thrust it on her head sideways, the tail dangling over one ear. She kicked off her shoes and sang: Born on a mountaintop in Tennessee/Killed a pig when I war three/Davy, Davy Crockett/King of the Wild Frontier.

Arnie put his hand over his eyes. Goldalee stamped and danced around him singing Davy Crockett, and when she came around in front of him again, she had taken the coonskin tail in her mouth and waggled it so it flapped against her full cheeks.

Through the cracks in his fingers, Arnie started to laugh. Then he cried. He took his hands down and slumped further into the chair, legs sprawled out, laughing and crying. She circled him, chanting: Davy—Big Tex—I'll get you yet—Beautiful Arnold Weingarten Crockett.

Arnie laughed and sobbed and thought he heard himself say: like hell you will.

She was whirling around him now, swinging the cap by the tail and smacking it against her flanks and backside, her face getting flushed, singing odd phrases, breathing harder.

Big Tex Weingarten, and she danced around him—

King of the Stockyards

I'll get you yet
King of the Jews
Beautiful Pig Lover

Then he got up from the chair and grabbed her wrist, wanting to stop this crazy dance, and she spun and whirled a few more times while he hung on to her waist, and she dropped the coonskin cap and he hugged her; she was scrunching down, her knees sagging so the top of her head barely came up to his chin; he almost had to hold her up and he held her tightly and they were both crying and Arnie didn't care if anyone saw two large people kissing and hugging and crying.

Decline and Fall

Ben read $18.91 on the supermarket register. His eyes blinked and kept fluttering so he tensed his ears, that sometimes worked, and the blinking stopped. Squeezing past the empty cart and craning his neck, he examined the register tape. What had gone wrong with his wife Ruth's infallible list? He had seen her carefully checking prices in the store's Red Special Ad and the total came to fourteen dollars and change. He had exactly three five-dollar bills in his wallet.

Take that back, Ben said, pushing the large tomato juice can away from his purchases. And these, and he pushed the tuna fish away and one can caught on the black roller and spun crazily on its side. Now he pushed away the ice milk, the kids loved it, and the frozen doughnuts, must have been dreaming to pick those up, and the pipe tobacco, another indulgence. How much, he said to the girl at the register.

The cashier added items on a paper bag, then discarded Ben's rejects into the wire cart next to her. She subtracted: $15.87, she announced.

Too much, he said, and blindly shoved other cans away.

You oughta count your stuff, the girl said, but Ben's fierce look stopped her mouth. He grabbed two dollars and loose change from the cashier, daring the next man in line to complain, and cradling the two large bags in both hands, he walked out.

On the way to the bus he stopped for a newspaper, had to put one bag of groceries down to grope for his change, and then with both bags in his arms, he waited for the no. 44. The paper lay folded on top of the two bags. It started to slide off, and Ben caught the newspaper with his chin and found himself staring into the plump face of Ethel-wife-spy-mother and the thin bespectacled face of Julius-consort-spy-father. No need to read the headline. EISENHOWER TURNS DOWN APPEAL OF ROSENBERG SPIES. Victims, Ben wanted to scream at them. Always, he had loathed the Ethel-Jewesses and avoided them in favor of long-legged, tall blond girls. He recoiled from the stoop-shouldered Juliuses. The ones whose caps were pushed over their eyes, the ones pushed against wet green-painted school fences, thrown into puddles, their balls stolen. He'd avoided them always. Better Louis Lepke Buchalter or Jacob Gurrah Shapiro, Gurrah for get out of here, fuck off, or you'll get a bellyful of hot Jewish gangster lead from my deadly jewish twin machine guns.

In the jouncing gassy chamber, Ben set the two bags down on an empty seat, only six other passengers this Saturday afternoon, and weaved his way forward to the driver to pay his fare. First bus ride for groceries in a long time, he thought, but fuel pump shot, tires gone, starter chintzy—he just had to junk the old green Plymouth, didn't have the two hundred bucks to put it into shape.

Ben leaned over and tried to raise his window. Let a bit of spring inside. Everything looked different through the unaccustomed bus window. He jammed the side clips down with both hands and heaved and strained and finally, in skips and hops, tore the window open. The bus stopped at Winfield Circle and Ben watched a man, smoking a cigar, pushing a rotary mower across his lawn at the busiest corner of the circle. The man was barefoot and Ben wondered how he'd manage if the mower caught his ten toes simultaneously and chopped them off. Could he live? How about five toes? Or two toes?

Then as the bus turned and entered sharply curving Seafoam Avenue, Ben examined his own behavior in the supermarket. Brownie points since he hadn't gotten too angry at the checkout girl. I'm not mad at Ruth for putting too many things on the list. I'm not mad at me for throwing extra items in the basket. I'm not the injustice collector I used to be just eight years ago. I'm not the defender of the faithful. I don't go around threatening to punch people because my overly keen ears heard them insult the Jews. Someone called him a bully once, said for anyone his size to go around threatening people wasn't risky. Not true, not true—he'd take anyone on, any size at all. Yes, he'd raised a rifle butt above a G.I's head but the guy deserved it. He'd do it again. Why hadn't the men he provoked beaten him up or tried to anyway? Simple answer: they had no cause. He had been the Messiah with the mission. Simple *meshigana*-crazy mission: while Hitler was efficiently exterminating Jews in Europe, no one, not any one, in Ben Cohen's hearing could insult the Jews.

Ben was alone in the bus when it pulled up at the last stop, where Wavecrest meets Seafoam Avenue. Across the street, his white asbestos-shingled house with green trim, and he spied Meyer Gurowski's yellow taxicab sitting out front. Ben walked past the mailbox and looked expectantly toward the little hummock where his two little girls had a private hollow space where they brought their dolls—he wanted the two of them to rise out of the hollow and run toward him. They did rise, but looked blankly as if they didn't recognize their father, turned and ran off into the woods behind the house, the quicksilver four-year-old, blond hair flying, and her dark sister, a year younger but the identical size, following unsteadily on pudgy legs.

Inside, he placed the two bags on the work counter. Ruth came in, and Ben heard Meyer G. roaring in the next room.

I fucked up the list, Ruth, Ben said, squeezing her upper arm.

You've picked up a new vocabulary, Ben. Please entertain my father. She started unpacking the groceries.

Ben brushed his lips against the back of his wife's head. Copper-colored hair, not the golden hair he had promised himself once; he rested one hand on the curve of her hip; his father-in-law was bellowing, coffee, coffee, coffee. I want coffee. This chant accompanied by rhythmic foot-stamping. The Blue Danube waltz on the record player skipped and chattered.

Turning away, Ben walked into the living-dining room. Stop it, Meyer. Ruth's preparing dinner. I'll get you a chunk of raw meat. You can chew on it while you're waiting.

All right, *chaver,* don't be so touchy. Meyer, his body clothed in happy, healthy fat, didn't get up but reached one hand out from the couch.

Ben gripped the out-thrust square hand. He knew that if the Russian Revolution had depended on Meyer, it would have failed when the Bolsheviks refused to forgo their holiday. Meyer insisted on summers in the Jewish colony in Bethlehem, New Hampshire (for his asthma), and boasted he kept teachers' hours and always brought his gypsy cab home by 3:00 P.M.

Ben sank into the walnut chair made to order for his large frame in their more affluent days. He gripped the arms. Pipe in mouth, he reached into his shirt pocket, then crumpled the empty tobacco pouch and balled it in his hand.

They're killing the Jews, from Meyer, taking his ease on the couch. The Rosenbergs and then the Gurowskis!

Cut it out.

Not you. You're dead already.

Ben clenched his fist on the cellophane pouch. It popped with a tiny pop.

So—Mr. Manager, *k'nocker,* you lost a good job.

I'm doing honest work, Meyer.

At half the pay. Beat the system, Ben. You're letting it beat you. Ruth told me. You were ready to punch your boss's head off. So they fired you. Get smart, boychick!

That's enough, Meyer!

Call me Mike! You'll beat me up now, if I don't keep quiet? I'm afraid so I'll keep quiet.

I'll give you that two hundred back. In a couple of weeks, if I get some overtime.

I don't need it yet. You'll give it back when I go to the country.

Ben heard the back door open. His youngest stole inside and sidled over to him, leaning against his legs.

To his granddaughter, as the child turned her back on him and hugged Ben's knees, oh you little beauty, with your mother's round brown eyes. I'll get the presents in just a minute. How's the factory, Ben?

A shot and a beer, Ben said, rubbing his hand through his daughter's close-cropped hair. His wife called out, dinner's ready. Meyer had never lost faith in the Revolution, and Ben marveled how Ruth had been able to survive, even bloom, under Meyer.

While Ben was sipping his second cup of coffee, he heard the horn signal that meant his car pool had arrived. Kisses all around, and he strained the two children to him. The horn blew again and as he turned to go, Meyer got up and thrust a wrinkled petition at him. Clemency for the Rosenbergs, Ben read, and dropped it on the work counter and dashed out the door. The old faker, he thought, hands out petitions, and runs off to the country right after Memorial Day.

Ben slid inside next to Gaetano Augeri, whose head barely cleared the steering wheel of his polished black Buick. Hated to go in today, but time and a half and he calculated another eighteen dollars added to his regular $63.50 take-home pay, ten cents an hour extra for second-shift differential, couldn't afford to miss it.

Gus said, did you get an early-bird matinee?

Got an early-bird father-in-law.

Tough shit. My wife put out. A reward for working on Saturday. I give her the overtime.

No, I give my old lady a rest on the weekend. Ruth should hear him now. And Julius—he visited Ethel the other day, wire-mesh screen and iron bars between them. Could he bang her, even now, if he had the chance?

The day, like all other days. Up to the old red-brick plant on Plane Street in the asshole of Newark, fewer men in today so you could get to the time clock without the shuffling lock-step of the weekdays, clock in at 4:30 P.M. sharp, screw around with the tweezers and soldering iron and calibrate five ammeters by 8 o'clock, inspector rejects one before supper break, buy coffee from the wagon and eat sandwich from home, surprise—piece of apple streusel too, wonder how to kill time from 8:30 until 1:00 A.M., go to john for fourth time and smoke inside, flush cigarette down, can't bum another from Gus, easier to smoke on Saturdays, only one foreman for three floors, recalibrate rejected meter and do three more, only 11 o'clock, guys get sore if you do more than eight meters. He remembered his early mistakes. On the first day in military packing, dipping the cartons into the warm amber wax, he had finished the night's quota in two hours. Gus put him wise. After three days, he stopped carrying the *New York Times* under his arm. This too made him conspicuous.

That night he insisted on a late-late show. Ruth complied. He wasn't sure she was even fully awake. Then she said, sleepily, when do I get a night off?

Bang—bang—bang.

Ben learned to distinguish the various floors of the plant by the sounds. The punch-press floor went bang—bang—bang. The operator presses on a treadle and releases the bit. Or he grabs two handles over his head and releases the bit. Over and over, he grabs. After three months in the plant, he heard this story from three different guys: See that fellow with two fingers missing on his right hand. He was trying to make time on the press and tied down one handle, so he could use one hand to drop the bit. Turn out more pieces. Pieces of ass. Vera the Vamp was always ready for a dry fuck in the carton-storage room. But keep out of her pants, she's happily married.

Julius hadn't had sex with Ethel for two years. Separate cells. Ethel wrote poetry. You'll be sorry, World, Julius told the World, just one hundred feet from Ethel in the Sing Sing condemned block. I shit on you and your kind, the World answered.

The floor with the lathes made a low swishing sound as scraps came off the machines like coiled springs that curled along the floor like many silver snakes. Vera walked past his bench. Flat-faced Vera never smiled and owned two sweaters, a pink cable-knit and a white angora; today she wore the white angora and her thighs rubbing together made a sound not unlike the lathes. Vera turned back and stood near Ben's bench, her eyes half closed. I'm so tired, she said, if only someone would just take me in their arms and rock me to sleep.

Ben shifted gears and banged Ruth early in the morning while the two kids were downstairs watching Betty Boop on the black Admiral television.

Summer approached and the plant windows couldn't be opened. They had never been opened.

Ben took the back staircase down one day to avoid Jolting Joe the Tree Man. Joe pruned trees in the daytime and worked Ben's shift at night. Ben heard Joe say, the Chair's too easy, I'd use the guillotine on them, and he made a chopping motion with his brawny forearm. On the second floor Ben discovered a new room. He peered inside. What's in there, he asked a guy walking out, pushing a cart filled with needle-like glittering chips. This was the maddest room of all—a jangling, head-banging, chaotic noise, no accountable rhythm to it. The smell of burning oil hit his nostrils.

Gus told him, driving home, those were the milling machines. Four guys in the car pool now. Gus needed the money and got three dollars apiece from each of them. On U.S. 1, traveling south, they passed the Budweiser plant every night. Through the large glass windows you could see huge vats as big as boilers, large valves as big as garbage-can covers, and tunnels of interconnecting pipes. High above the plant an eagle appeared in red neon lights against a yellow-lit background. The red lights would flash and disappear and reappear and the eagle flapped its red wings and then all grew dark.

Gus said, every night, the eagle's flying high tonight.

Pop Delaney, the millwright, thirty years in the plant, right pinky missing, answered, every single night, watch out, or it'll shit right in your eye.

Ben realized after a while that they protected themselves with ritual. On Friday, payday, they all stopped for a beer in Willicks. No one had much to say and each man bought a round before they headed for home.

Ben found his life reversed. He banged Ruth every night, rarely missing, but never on Saturday or Sunday.

Ben saw a picture of the sallow-faced Rosenberg attorney walking away from Sing Sing with a little boy on either side. The children had ringed eyes and peaked thin faces.

Time was getting very short; they had Ben where his hair was short.

Ben looked under Ruth's silverware tray in the kitchen one night. Ruth cut out recipes and stored them here. Also Ruth was not the kind of girl to throw anything away. Not anything important. He found the Clemency for the Rosenbergs petition under a recipe for apple streusel.

That night Ruth spoke. You've changed from boxer shorts to those tight sexy ones. Why?

They're cooler in the summertime.

But where did you get the money?

The sound in the punch-press room had changed recently from bang—bang—bang to boom—boom—boom. I love you, Ruth, Ben said, as he pressed her to him. They broke apart and looked out the bedroom window, the five-pointed gum tree leaves so thick now that the streetlight shone dark green. A slight breeze came through the screen. Maybe this early heat wave will break soon, Ben thought. A branch stirred, then another waving its star-shaped leaves, and the wind opened a path through the high limbs; the light appeared yellow and flickering; the rain spattered down against the leaves, large fat drops, more wind. Ben kissed Ruth again, standing before the open window, in his shorts, enjoying the breeze and spatter of rain against his chest.

Ben and Ruth sat, side by side, on the edge of the bed facing the window. Ruth lay back first, and then Ben had to crawl over her to his place near the wall; the children still quiet in the next room; thunderclaps and they listened for the children's voices. Ruth took Ben's hand as they lay side by side, saying thanks Ben, for a lovely night off.

The following day, after Gus parked the car, Ben waited for the other two to leave, and he tested the Clemency petition on Gus. In a quiet voice he said, think of their two kids. Gus signed, without a word. In the Meter Testing Department Ben approached a few others, and in a short time he got four more signatures. He avoided Jolting Joe and cornered Vera in the carton room. She signed and asked Ben to wait for her husband tomorrow and she'd see that he signed too.

Back to his bench, he plugged in the soldering iron and sat down.

Dick Murray, the Seton Hall law student, peered over Ben's shoulder. You'll get into trouble, Ben, if the foreman sees you.

Not so loud, Dick.

You'll get into trouble, Dick said, even louder.

Ben arose, put his right hand over the petition, and balled his left into a fist.

Lots of bad trouble, Dick shouted down the length of the aisle.

Fuck off, Dick. Ben cocked his fist.

If you hit me, I'll hit back. Also, you'll lose your job and go to jail.

You want me to lose my job, Dick? Ben folded the petition and stuffed it in his rear pocket.

That's up to you, Ben, and Dick walked away.

The eagle stopped flying a few days later. A blackout. If the power failure extended all the way to Ossining—Friday, Ben got on the long line at the bar and paid twenty-five cents to cash his check. He needed the money to pay for his round of beers at Willicks. The third car-pool passenger signed; Pop Delaney said: they got what they deserved. The eagle flew again but the flying wings flapped more quickly. At least Ben thought so but he didn't mention this to the others.

Not a breath of air that last night, sweat poured down Ben's forehead, sweat behind his ears, acid sweat on his neck. He mopped and soldered the little wires together. He placed his crumpled handkerchief next to him on the bench. Then he went to the bathroom and wet it in the sink and brought it back to wipe his face and the back of his neck. His elbow brushed the sodden handkerchief to the dirty floor. He left it there. The loudspeaker announced: Julius and Ethel are spending their last evening together. The inspector returned six ammeters, all rejected. Ben started again on the first reject. He grasped the wire with the tweezers. Fanny the Giraffe, four benches away and on the other side of the divider, said, we'll have fried Rosenbergs soon. She giggled, then laughed and choked on the laugh. Ben took the soldering iron in his hand and applied it to the blond hair on his forearm. The hair sizzled; smelled like nothing else he had ever smelled before. He burned a swath through the hair from wrist to elbow.

The radio announced: one hour left. They're back in their cells and they are preparing them. Who prepares them? It grew very still. All heads bent down to the work at the benches. Ben recalibrated two meters and pushed them aside. His elbow on the bench, he rotated the soldering iron in a slow circle. The loudspeaker brayed: "When the Saints Go Marching In." Three women fainted in Union Square. One half hour to go, the solemn radio voice announced. One more announcement: President Eisenhower denied last clemency appeal. Ben remembered the Clemency petition with seven signatures was still in the kitchen drawer.

Ben sensed someone near him, over him. Jolting Joe said, your friends will get it soon. What they deserve. They'll fry!

Ben sprang to his feet. I'll put your eyes out, son-of-a-bitch. He thrust the soldering iron at Joe's eyes. Joe leaped back, then halted, his thumbs hooked onto his broad woodchopper's belt.

Ben advanced on him, holding the iron face-high. I'll blind you, you bastard. Then you'll be able to see. You'll see. See! See! See! The male end of the iron pulled out of the workbench outlet.

Gus came careening around the other end of the bench. Ben threw the iron on the concrete floor. It slid and stopped in front of Joe's treeman boots. The inspector held Joe by the arm and talked to him in a low voice. Gus stood in front of Ben, leaning into him, both hands embracing his waist, Gus's head under Ben's left armpit.

Ben drooped, limp now, his weight resting on his little friend's back. He'd have seared Joe before; now he couldn't. Maybe not ever again.

They pulled the switch. First Julius, then Ethel a few minutes later.

Ben's eyes blinked furiously. Joe had disappeared. Gus led Ben to the washroom. He handed Ben a cigarette. He lit it for him. Ben puffed inside the toilet stall. He retched in the bowl. Dropped the cigarette into the bowl, got down on his knees and heaved again. And again, but nothing came out.

On the way home, they passed the Budweiser plant and the eagle flapped its wings as usual. But no one said, it'll shit right in your eye. No one said anything.

Ben got out, heard Gus's more O.T. Ben, see you tomorrow, and he saw a light in his bedroom window. When he came upstairs, Ruth put down the book she'd been reading.

Strange things happened all night, he said.

Tell me. I heard it's all over.

I crept into Ethel's cell, past the guards. I had sex with her. I spirited her out—you know—if I had the wings of an angel, over these prison walls I would fly.

You couldn't, you're lying.

Yes, I'm lying. Strange things happened. I tried to blind a man.

You're lying.

Yes, I'm lying.

A strange night. You remember Vera the Vamp, the one with the big tits?

You never mentioned her large breasts.

I told you about her. Her husband comes off the day shift when she comes on my second shift. They have long conversations. About domestic things. What she left for dinner. How to warm it up. What the kids did in school that day. She brushed against me on the way out. She stopped in front of me, saying, I'm so tired. I wish someone would take me in their arms and rock me to sleep. I thought I'd faint from the smell of her.

I've got that cramp in my calf again, Ruth said. She stiffened. Then she raised her right leg and placed the sole flat on the bed. Tried to reach her right calf with her hand, but gave up and stretched both legs out again.

O.K., O.K. Lie still. I'll take care of it. He bent over her and kneaded the muscles with both hands until he felt the calf muscle loosening and she relaxed. He kissed her on the cheek. I'm ashamed, he said, but I need a woman.

She started to get out of bed.

Where are you going?

To get my diaphragm.

No. You don't need it.

She sat on the edge of the bed, her feet on the floor.

Ben put his arm around her shoulders and drew her down, to his side. He joined to her.

An act of faith.

La Causa

I'm caught by the red light at Houston and the Bowery. The hairy ape, scornful mouth, sticks his cupped hand through my rolled-down car window. Save me from a life of crime, mister, the kid says, knuckles resting on my horn. I fasten my thumb and index finger on his filthy shirt cuff, yank his hand up, and shove it through the window, quickly rolling the window closed.

The lights turn green as he swipes at the windshield with a dirty rag; a film of grease obscures my vision, and I gun the car; too fast, almost smack the rear fender of the car in front. I jam the brakes, stall; impatient honks behind me and I restart the car and head for the Holland Tunnel. I pump the windshield-cleaner button but no water comes out and I turn into the tunnel mouth, craning my neck around the poor unfortunate's vengeance—the black axle-grease smear. I could have given him a dime. It's not against my principles. Sometimes I give, dimes or quarters, sometimes not. Yet it does no good.

At home in Jersey dinner's over, and I search for suitable office tidbits for my wife.

She comes right to the point. I had lunch out today. For dessert, a bunch of luscious ruby grapes. She waits. I nod. Because of you our kids haven't tasted grapes in eight years!

After all—they haven't been home in three months.

And lettuce, they don't know what lettuce tastes like either.

You can get the Aztec brand, the strike's over. But no Teamsters' lettuce or grapes. That's out!

Where can I find it?

Use spinach leaves, very nutritious, escarole—

I'm sick of them.

I'll plant leaf lettuce again like last year. Just give me a chance. Next year, I'll—I'll take you out to dinner, tomorrow.

Your lettuce was dirty, buggy, filthy. I threw it out!

Let's skip the coffee, it's too hot, and I fly upstairs to examine my junk mail. It is my custom to open letters daily but save magazine subscriptions, bills, ads, and fund appeals for once a week. I'm a donator. Give ten dollars, five dollars, never less than two dollars. Always by check.

During the Newark riots, I formed an Interracial Committee for Open Housing and Better Understanding. I put myself on the line! We persuaded a number of homeowners to remove the black coachmen, holding lanterns, that graced their front lawns. Also, we set up a special black history section in the local library. My dark black neighbor, Mr. Spencer, had no coachman but he removed his concrete donkey with two planters on either side and the large red-topped mushroom sheltering a green concrete turtle under it. One of my four committeemen, Mr. Spencer said, if those Newark no-accounts come out this way, I'll load my shotgun and fill 'em full of buckshot. Imagine!

A couple of years ago, I cut the Blacks when someone in CORE, I forget who, bad-mouthed the Jews. But later when Joan Little stabbed a white prison guard when he tried to rape her, I forgave the Blacks and sent ten dollars for her defense. I'm back on all the lists again and the appeals pour in: Poverty Law Center, NAACP Legal Defense Fund, CORE, Black Sanitation Workers of New Orleans. Also: Grape Workers, Lettuce Workers, Coal Miners' Reform Committee, Elect a Liberal Congress, United Jewish Appeal, Help the Russian-Jewish Emigrés; Lenny Bernstein asks, Congresswoman Bella Abzug wants, Senator Kennedy suggests, Sierra Club, and lots more.

I slit open the envelopes and find:

After a while, they disconnected the wire from my finger and

connected it to my ear. They immediately gave a high dose of
electricity. . . .

Send check to: Amnesty International

Great God!

I believe if guns are outlawed, murderers and thieves will
have control of our lives and property. We will have no defense.

National Rifle Association

Nuts!

I, the undersigned, petition the governments of Japan and
Russia, and all other countries engaged in commercial whale-
killing, to put an immediate stop to the needless slaughtering of
whales.

Please make check payable to:
THE WHALE PROTECTION FUND

So!

When she returned home. Doug, her fourteen-year-old son,
was opening his Valentine's Day mail on the drainboard of the
kitchen sink. She shot him in back of the head. She found Lucy,
eleven years old, in her bedroom and killed her with a single
shot too.

Send check to: National Coalition
to Ban Handguns

Too much!

A little over five years ago my daughter, Allison, and three
other students were killed by National Guard rifle fire at Kent
State University. In addition, thirteen others were shot and in-
jured—one permanently paralyzed.

A special note from: Arthur S. Krause.
Send check to: Kent State Due Process
of Law Fund

I can't stand it!

I stack the current appeals in a neat pile to my right. Above my desk, I paste meaningful pictures and/or quotations until they out-live their usefulness. I look up at the tear-stained, Jewish face of Naomi Rodstein of Queens Village, New York, her face contorted with grief when she heard the news of the crash of the C-54 army transport carrying 243 Vietnamese orphans on their way to the United States. I had to borrow my wife's cuticle scissors to cut the picture from the newspaper. My wife leaned on my shoulder as I snipped. Who can blame her for crying, she said. When I cry, you finally do what I want—the right thing. I shuffle the fund appeals. Tear the envelopes into little pieces and throw the scraps into the wastebasket. Cast away the Rifle Association and Whales appeals and check my bank balance. I place the three remaining appeals into the third drawer on the right-hand side of the desk; they join eight or ten appeals left over from the last two weeks. All worthwhile ones. Important.

I pay the meat bill, scavenger bill, drug bill. Pay my daughter's dental bill, mortgage, Wallach's ninety-day charge, phone bill, gas bill, electric bill, car payment. Jolly little money left! Tear Naomi Rodstein's picture off the wall; replace it with a quotation from Eugene O'Neill, seeking new inspiration.

I'm still with my dilemma: what to give? I remember a Jewish girl, friend of my daughter, who traveled all the way to Santo Domingo to bring back a small, brown baby and named him Avram. And then she wanted a second and purchased a Panamanian and called him David. Who else but a Jewish girl would deliberately raise two brown babies, three and seven months old. They are good now, Avram and David, but how they'll cry when they grow up.

On the way to work, the following day, I look for the bushy-haired windshield swiper. All gone now, the teeny boppers and hippies making the scene. Park my car and stride down Houston Street. The turf's been reclaimed by the original settlers: the Men's Shelter bums and harmless winos. First Avenue and Houston after a rain-storm: steam rises from the asphalt like a tropical rain forest: grape-fruit halves, mangos, newspapers, rags, and beer cans clog the storm

drain. I walk past the black park attendant sweeping in front of the
bocci court, swivel past the white drunk who lurches toward me, and
taking a short running jump, I leap the river of garbage; too short
with my left foot and I step into the muck which slops into my shoe.
There he is! I think it's the same ugly: watery blue eyes, dirt-
smudged forehead, hair all over his face. The bum sticks his hand
out.

Maybe it's not the same one. They look alike. Who cares? Luckily,
I've caught one of the last of the breed. My own son is safely in
school. I bought his way out with a hard-fought, expensive college
deferment. This bushy-head drops his hand and sways like a
Talmud Student. My son's on his way to a Ph.D. in anthropology.
No problems there—he can study primitive peoples, Panamanians
and Patagonians. Exploring a site, he may find Patagonians and
Panamanians in unambiguous stratigraphic association and then report back to us.

Got any change, the boy says. He's a throwback, I think, an
anachronism with that old jive hippy talk.

Come with me, I say to the boy. I won't give you a handout but if
you're hungry, I'll buy you breakfast.

Dad, he screams! I love you, Dad. And he throws his arms around
me.

Never mind that, I say, breaking his arms apart, smelling the
dried urine smell of him. Just follow me.

He trails me across East Second Street and past the oasis
of corner laundromat, East Side Italian bakery, and Luz Spanish-
American restaurant; they sweep and hose their storefronts, and
with the kid a half-step behind, we cross East Third to Ukrainian
Lisa's red-front luncheonette. I motion him inside, and as he opens
the door a purple sweater sails out of a window three floors up; a
small boy below catches the sweater, and simultaneously a flower pot
falls at my feet scattering dirt and one pink geranium. Look what
you made me do, a woman screams and slams the window down. I
marvel at my luck: I could have suffered Cyrano's fate under that
pot. Now my bum is backing out of the luncheonette and I take his
arm and guide him back in. Sit down!

All right, Dad

Don't call me Dad! What would you like? Scrambled eggs, toast, and coffee O.K.?

I don't serve that kind here, mister, Lisa says, hands folded across her bosom.

Come on, Lisa. You know me. I'll pay for his breakfast.

No. I don't want that trade.

My charge starts to cry, wiping his eyes with his sleeve. Dad, I'm a bum, nothing but a bum, and little Mom won't even serve me breakfast. I'm starving.

My hand hovers above his shoulder, can't bring it down.

He blubbers, I'm a goner. A bum. A bum. A bum.

Father Dominic told me what a good woman you are, Lisa. Make him a fried egg on roll and coffee to go. He'll eat it outside. Here's a dollar. I glance at my watch. This took longer than I thought and I'm late for work. The kid's crying into his cupped hands. Is he putting me on? He's peering between his fingers at me. His tears look real. I look through his finger lattice from my side: bitten nails and a missing pinky joint on his left hand; how did he lose it? Only nine nails left. When Lisa stuffs my dollar into her apron pocket and then cracks an egg onto the griddle, I turn and walk out, calling back, so long, Son, but I don't wait for his reply.

My office measures eight by twelve feet. Desk takes up three by four feet; safe two by two feet. Double-tiered gun-metal IN box on left, OUT box on right. Eight corncob pipes in two ashtrays. Four of the pipes' bowls are so charred that if I light one of these by mistake, it catches fire. Yet I don't throw them out. The air conditioner blows icy blasts on my neck.

The plump woman shrinks back into the green, steel-framed chair, whispers, I can't pay the rent.

What's the trouble?

Do you know Jewish?

I nod.

He's seventy-two and he left me. I took in my sister-in-law when her husband died. He said in the Bible it is written you should do this. With my sister-in-law he went off. I don't know where he's gone. Maybe Florida. We worked together for forty-five years in the grocery. He's gone—

If I look up, I see the room's only picture thumbtacked to the wall: an artist's proof, brown earth, blue sky, two rumpled gray hills, framed in white matboard.

You're not listening!

I press the recorder inside me and repeat word for word her last three sentences. She seems satisfied. Go to the Friendship Center on Avenue A and East Seventh, I tell her. I offer a referral card. Maybe they can help you.

She sighs, a giant sigh that ruffles the papers on my desk.

I sigh too.

Fingering the card, she gets up and half turns, saying, can they bring him back? She goes through the doorway and I see the card fluttering to the floor. I turn off the air conditioner.

I phone my plastic-bag vendor. Take those eighteen rolls back, I say. They tear apart. The garbage spills all over the street because of your lousy bags. I slam the receiver down. It's too quiet. I can hear my own voice. I turn on the air conditioner. It rumbles in the small room.

I dash out of the office to the bank. Turn back to pick up my bumbershoot, left open to dry in the storeroom. Twirl the umbrella in an arc to dispel the miasmic humors of my office. I cross Avenue A to trek down Godfather II street. Not too long ago, Hollywood rented the street and dressed the storefronts in green-and-white awnings, hung arty 1920s signs and multicolored pennons; for a short while, the street turned into one long Feast of San Gennaro, the sidewalks swept and the people walking past the Fotografia Italiana and Farmacia Italiana, all happier, gayer, laughing, and less treacherous.

I pass the windowless Consolidated Edison generating plant. A small white butterfly ignores the signs HIGH VOLTAGE—DANGER—NO TRESPASSING in English and Spanish and flies through the spiked green gate into the hum of the generators. There's the squat figure of Ukrainian Lisa far down the street and I hurry to catch up with her. Did she give the boy his egg sandwich?

Across the street is the gleaming, white enameled storefront gym, a silhouette of a muscular black man flexing biceps in the window. Slash, slash the heavy air with my umbrella. If a knife artist lunged at me, I could flick the umbrella open, riposte, catch the knife in the umbrella folds, flip it out of the mugger's hands, and then—

Pass a building, door and windows covered with galvanized sheet iron and sign: BEWARE OF DOGS; next door, a small lettered sign on the bell-lobby door: HOT WATER TODAY, FOLKS—KI-YIPPY-YI—Sign up for baths. The Hollywood storefronts are fading, papers blowing, bands of loafers (what are they called: the unemployed, the welfare chiselers, the disadvantaged, the under-privileged, I don't know any longer) on every stoop. My shirt sticks to my back. I walk into the gutter to avoid an open gushing hydrant. I'm catching up to Lisa now and I see it's not her but a taller, bulkier woman wearing a babushka and carrying a shopping bag. Two men have sidled in front of her. I know their game: confrontation pan-handling. She moves to the right and they move with her. She can't pass. One man wears a denim jacket and leather bush hat pulled over his face; the other has on a hooded navy sweatshirt and carries a knobkerry: four feet of black pipe with a threaded T-bar handle. I halt at the far edge of the hydrant's spray, standing in the runoff. I hope they're not Blacks. I like Blacks. Hard luck, the hooded guy turns his head. He is black. I walk toward the curb, pass behind the woman, and I grasp her elbow. Come with me, dear, I say, I'll walk you to the corner.

Hooded man turns on me. What are you doing here, honky? I step back. My heart's beating ninety miles a minute. He sweeps his cane at me and I duck; it whistles overhead. He prances toward me, the cane held sword fashion, and I step back, back, then flip my umbrella button and the black shield opens in front of me. One sweep of his cane and the umbrella is torn from my hand, goes sail-ing off. He jabs. I step back into the water and now I'm standing ankle-deep in the hydrant flow. I see clearly. The woman has dis-appeared. Two men, heads bent, are playing cards on the nearest stoop. They don't look up. My assailant is wearing blue canvas sneakers; the other fellow hasn't moved; he has platform shoes.

Your wallet, chuck it here, the hooded man says. Fast, Man!

Muggers mug at night. He broke the rules. I can't scream/yell.

He flips his cane in the air, catches the ferrule end, and takes a golf swing, spraying water over me with the mallet end.

I'm assaulted by the urge to piss. Hold it in. The moment passes, and using the quick-draw technique (had practiced it often), I slip my hand into my right trouser pocket, fasten on my wallet, and with one motion, toss it toward him. He catches it against his chest, turns and lopes toward B. Cowboy trails him on platform shoes like a man on stilts.

I look for help. No one. The card players have disappeared. The street's deserted. I slosh through the water toward Avenue B. Then I remember they have my check so no reason to go to the bank. Turn back toward A. If I pass a police car—none pass by and I head for the Ninth Precinct station, change my mind and walk to the parking lot. My shoes squish. Getting in my car, I drive toward the Holland Tunnel, expecting to be stopped for driving without my license.

I'm home. Go to the cabinet over the wall oven and reach for the Canadian Club. My wife places her fingers over my biceps, saying, you don't need it. My, you're home early. How about a glass of vermouth on the rocks, twist of lemon. It's cooling. .

I pull away and pour a double or fourple and chuck it down. Good warm stomach burn.

I go up the stairs, bent double and grasping the stair treads in front of me, climbing a ladder; then, halfway up, I go down on my hands and knees (ignoring my old mother's dictum, change your pants when you get home from school), maybe I can tear the pants or regain my football bursitis, it's not fatal.

What are you doing? my wife hollers up the staircase.

Carry on, I shout back. Must call my office. I'll be right down. Now I yell louder but no sound comes out. I wish he wasn't black. Splitting headache. I crawl the rest of the way up the stairs. Still on hands and knees, I creep to my den and shove the door open. I grab my chair and hoist myself into it.

Over my desk, tear off the latest quotation, from Eugene O'Neill this time; don't read it, whatever it is or was, I need a new one! Open my checkbook. My account is overdrawn but nonetheless I write three ten-dollar checks and send them out to three causes. Stamp the envelopes with the commonest stamp of all, The Liberty Bell, and notice for the first time on this modest stamp, the slogan: PRO-CLAIM LIBERTY THROUGHOUT ALL THE LAND. It will have to do.

For a while.

The Reckoning

This was the fourth funeral I had attended in two years and the third time my name had been called as a pallbearer. My aunts and uncles were dying, and funeral directors were hard-pressed to select able-bodied men among the survivors to carry the casket. The casket was placed on a rubber-wheeled cart and the pallbearers walked alongside, touching the coffin in a ceremonial manner.

This time we had to carry Uncle Jack, whom I recalled as a small, wiry man who filled my adolescence with intense discussions and many family quarrels. My uncle seemed unexpectedly heavy as we carried the casket to the waiting hearse.

A red-headed, excitable man, he could never sit in one place for more than a few minutes. He was always out of his chair, pacing, waving a finger in the air at my stolid father, who would listen patiently, then shake his head in disagreement as Jack pounded his left fist into his palm.

He never finished high school. His first job was buggy-lugging dresses in the crowded garment center; then he sold shoes. Later my father took him into the painters' union, but he soon gave that up to drive a cab and tried to organize the drivers into a union of their own. All this time, he denounced the capitalist oppressors, extolled the Communist party, and sold subscriptions to the *Daily Worker*.

I loved Jack, my father's youngest brother, almost more than I loved my hardworking father. From the time I was five or six years old, I remember Jack giving me a nickel every time he came to the house. He continued handing out nickels, without realizing his nephew was growing up and inflation had set in. At sixteen, embarrassed, I would surreptitiously pocket the nickel while Jack argued with my father and finally persuaded him to take a trial subscription to the *Sunday Worker.*

Jack didn't deliver the *Worker* carefully wrapped like contraband. No, he would ride his bicycle past our Flatbush two-family house and throw it unwrapped against the front door as though it was the *New York Times.* The defiant thump of the newspaper against the door adjoining the sun parlor where I slept would awaken me. If I pulled up the shade, Jack would be out there, standing astride his bike, a few more papers in his rear carrier.

"Come on out, Lennie. Get your bike! Don't waste the day in bed." He started calling me Lennie when I was six or so, and the name Lazar disappeared.

My father canceled the paper. He could not bear seeing the naked headline U.S. IMPERIALISM DYING exposed to the neighbors' scrutiny.

We deposited Jack in the hearse. I returned to the parking lot, where my father and his sister Fannie joined me for the ride to Mt. Zion cemetery. Car lights went on and the meager cortege lined up to follow the hearse.

We passed solid brick homes, their fronts abloom with masses of pink and red azaleas. The white-petaled dogwood blossoms were already turning brown at the edges, curling inward, and falling onto the clipped green lawns.

Aunt Fannie, sitting upright like a firmly corseted Buddha, rolled down the window to take deep breaths of fresh air.

Along crowded Queens Boulevard, we turned into a side street, turned again, then were caught by a truck and a red light. The hearse was out of sight.

"I think I'm lost," I said.

"Well, so," Aunt Fannie said, "It's a gorgeous day for a drive."

"Don't rush, Lennie," my father joined in. "Poor Jack was always rushing. Where he's going, he'll be a long time, so just drive carefully."

Our car caught up as the hearse turned onto the Long Island Expressway and we stayed close as the procession rolled past Bayside, Great Neck, and out toward Babylon.

Driving automatically, as the car followed the monotonous highway, I found it hard to imagine that this thin old man in the black jacket (and pants? Do they bury them in pants?) and dark tie could have been part of such Homeric times. *No pasaran.* The International Brigade. *La Pasionaria.*

I remember Jack saying, now you're old enough, Lennie, I must tell you how I got to Spain. Have a cigarette. No thanks, I said.

The battle was joined in 1936, Jack began. The Falangists, with help from Hitler and Mussolini, wanted to smash the duly elected Republican government of Spain. I had to go. We waited in France for three months. Twenty Americans, as many Germans, and a half-dozen Englishmen. Waited, waited, getting more anxious every day as groups of three to six men were called and slipped over the border. I drank wine, walked the streets, baked in the sun, chased girls. Don't believe those liars who tell you about the peasant girls dying to lay in the fields with the brave Americans of the Abraham Lincoln Brigade. Maybe a waitress, or a shop girl here and there. Finally I got my orders to pull out.

The party rep introduced me to a tiny American comrade, asked me to help her over the border, a black-haired, fine-boned little thing. She represented the labor press and a few small radical papers. Large, round, plum-colored eyes.

The French guardhouse and the Spanish one were three hundred yards apart. You couldn't see the Spanish checkpoint over the next hill. The border was closed, the Spanish checkpoint still in Loyalist hands, but instructions said not to let anyone over unless they had documents with eight signatures and seals. Impossible to get. Confusion. Rivalry. The Anarchists were afraid of the Communists and the Republican government distrusted both. They all wanted us to fight for them but were afraid to let us in.

So we waited. Waited until reliable men were in the Spanish checkpoint and we could go over. In the meantime, the girl and I walked up the dusty road to visit the three bored French soldiers in the guard station. Bring them a bottle of wine and talk. The girl could speak French fluently. I couldn't follow her as she jabbered at the soldiers and they joked and laughed, their three rifles stacked in a corner of the hut. The fifth visit, they invited us to share their lunch of bread and cheese and wine. While we were eating, a truck pulled up. A civilian in black suit coat, old blue pants, and a beret jumped off and took the tall French corporal aside. The corporal said, finish your lunch, *mes amis*. Today, you go. We'll hurry back and get our bags, I said. No time. You must leave now, the corporal said. These shoes, the girl said, pointing to her open sandals. I can still remember, Jack said, pausing to light another cigarette, her toes were coated with a fine gray dust.

We had our money in moneybelts strapped under our clothes and we piled into the front of the truck, the civilian driving, the corporal, the girl, and myself squeezed into the cab. We drove the short distance to the Spaniards. The corporal bent down and kissed her goodbye on top of her head, calling her the brave little one. Out came two Spaniards, each with a rifle carelessly held in one hand.

"Take good care of our friends," the corporal said, in Spanish. He got back into the truck where the civilian waited, the motor running. In a daring maneuver, as the rear wheels spun over open space, they turned the truck around and drove off.

"Where are you going?" the older Spaniard asked.

"To the *corrida*," I replied.

"Why?"

"To see the black bulls of Pamplona."

"Go ahead, then. Long live the Republic of Spain."

That was all. We walked away from the guardhouse up the hill, not looking back. Walking slowly, passing under a tree, the only tree on that rocky path, when a shot rang out. A few more shots that cut through the leaves overhead. I grabbed the girl's arm and we started to run. Her sandal fell off. Ping. A bullet hit a rock near us and I dragged her off the road into a field. We lay down on our bellies in the coarse grass. Brown from the sun and drought. I kissed her hard on the mouth. The first time. Glad to be alive. Never found out why they'd fired. After a few minutes, we rolled farther away from the road. I made a makeshift sandal from my shirttail and tied the cloth around her little foot. We walked—she leaned on me—until we passed the next two slopes; you could see them like camel's humps against the sky. Did you ever walk not up a hill but alongside one, one foot always higher than the other? Cows graze this way with no trouble. Walked a mile this way, paralleling the road, then a short scramble up the bank and we strolled into town to find our friends.

"What was the girl's name?" I asked.

"Selma."

If he had said Renata or Dolores or even Maria, I would have been sure he was lying, but when he said Selma, I believed him. Jack could dig up a more romantic name if he were lying. Selma, he said. It must be true.

Some years ago, Jack took me to a Carnegie Hall benefit for Loyalist refugees who escaped after Franco's victory and introduced me to some ex-Lincoln Brigaders. Collectively fat and balding, now teachers, lawyers, salesmen, they looked like they belonged at an American Legion meeting or a teachers' convention—it was hard to imagine them as The Immortals.

In a last desperate counterattack, the Loyalists climbed out of the trenches surrounding Madrid. They were civilians who had just finished breakfast, kissed their wives and children, put on their business suits or hunting jackets, and reported for duty. There was hardly a complete uniform among them. Only the two-pointed field caps and rifles they were rapidly firing as they ran toward the fascist lines identified them as soldiers. They ran on, fell down; got up, fell down. Some rose and ran again; others remained where they had fallen. Jack, the black beret purchased before he left New York still jammed on his head, brown tweed jacket over the blue work shirt, running and firing with the others. Running and firing. Running and firing.

My uncle returned from Spain, disenchanted with the Communist party, searching for new gods. He came to visit and told me he had joined the Socialist Labor party, which he now realized was taking the correct road.

"Lennie," he said, "come to a meeting. You'll see. Look at you. Tall and strong. We need you. College is fine but not enough."

I tried, really tried, enduring my older brother's taunts, half comprehending the lengthy arguments in a bare loft above a tavern in Red Hook. Jack was working in the garment center again, vague about his job; he talked about organizing hospital workers. One day he came to me and said he was leaving the Socialist Labor party and forming another group with a real revolutionary philosophy at last.

"How many people in this new group, Jack?"

"Well," he replied, "there are two of us in Chicago and I'm going out to the Coast where I've been promised a job with the Longshoremen's Union, Harry Bridges's outfit. I thought you could help organize in New York and we would all keep in touch."

"That's how many people, Jack?"

"Well," he grinned, "four, with you."

When Jack told my father his plans, calling Pop "Wullie"—the name he always used, instead of Bill or William, when he wanted my father to understand him, for old times' sake—not mentioning his own new revolutionary part, just the growing Longshoremen's Union, my father said, "You're still chasing her, Jacob."

"Not at all, Wullie," he said. "What in the hell made you bring that up?"

"I'm no fool, Jack," my father said. "I read the papers. First she took up with the writer. A good man. He didn't talk when the committee called him for questioning."

Jack's eyes narrowed and he bit his lower lip.

"That she left him," my father said, "never married him, I don't care. Who knows what goes on between a man and a woman. But I saw her picture in the paper with the new one, the labor lawyer, when he was called before the committee a year later. He talked. Named names."

"A rat," Jack said. "She cracked up. She's in a hospital in L.A. She needs me."

"Jack," my father said, "she's a clever woman. You're not clever."

I couldn't bear to look at my uncle. "You're decent. You're intelligent. You're kind, too kind, you worry about the whole world—but you're not clever."

Jack remained silent for a moment, then he jumped up and ran into the bathroom. He came out with a rose-colored towel draped over his arm like a cape, and with the lower half of my fishing rod for a sword he executed several passes at a ladder-back kitchen chair. *El Toro,* he shouted and stamped his feet. Flashed the bath towel and teased the bull to charge. Then avoided the sharp horns with a twisting, graceful movement of his hips. I yelled *ole, ole* and joined him— out of loyalty, so he wouldn't be embarrassed by the charade; galloping around the black bull, taller than my uncle at seventeen, I goaded it to a fighting fury with a broomstick.

My father laughed and my brother too. Even Mom smiled. After a few minutes I couldn't stand it anymore, seeing Jack play the clown, so I knocked the chair over with a sweep of the broom and hurried to the bathroom to run cold water over my flushed face.

I didn't join Jack's group. He left for the Coast and our family never saw him again. A few letters far apart; he promised many times to return for a visit but never made it.

We arrived at the cemetery, parked the car, and straggled up and down narrow lanes looking for the marked location. At last, Area Four, Section Seven. We went slowly along the paths searching for a newly dug grave. A few daffodils, flowers gone now, green stalks drooping, had forced their way through the ground near the headstones. Spying an open grave, I led the small group of mourners off the cinder path, our feet trampling spiny chestnut husks into the spongy turf.

The few relatives and friends huddled together beside the freshly turned earth while the bearded rabbi chanted.

On a spring day twenty-five years ago, Jack persuaded me to cut classes and join a noon picket line outside a Harlem hospital. I got out of the subway, walked a few blocks, and there was my uncle walking with six or eight Negro women whose white attendants' uniforms peered out from beneath their worn dark coats.

"Lennie, take this sign, I'll get another," Jack smiled at me proudly. "It's my nephew," he announced.

I grabbed the picket sign which said JIM CROW MUST GO. Jack took another from a small pile on the sidewalk which read UNION RECOGNITION NOW. We walked for ten or fifteen minutes and gradually the crowd swelled to about thirty—mostly Negroes and mostly women.

Jack chanted, "Jim Crow Must Go."

The congregation picked up the chant and repeated it over and over again. The sound heartened them and their tired gait quickened. The picketers began to step out in a marching rhythm.

A burly uniformed guard came out of the hospital gate and walked over to Jack. "You can't march here, blocking the entrance."

The picketers stopped and milled about uncertainly. A strongly built Negro woman stepped forward and stood alongside Jack. I moved to Jack's right, a pace behind. "We stay right here," she said. "This is our lunch hour." With a wave of her hand to the others, "Keep walking, sisters, pay him no mind."

The guard ignored her and addressed Jack. "Better get your people out of here. Move back one hundred feet from the entrance."

"We have a right to walk here," Jack said.

The guard clamped his hand on Jack's shoulder. "Now don't cause trouble, just move on."

He stood his ground, my uncle. A professional. He looked relaxed and contented as he waited under the guard's hand. And I'm at my uncle's right hand. *No pasaran.* I feel great. Then deliberately, Jack reached up and thrust the guard's hand away. The guard pulled a whistle from his pocket and blew blast after blast.

The rabbi's voice rose to a crescendo, then dropped and glided into silence.

There was a group a little removed from the other mourners—three men surrounding a woman. One of these men approached my father, touched his arm, and said, "Selma would like to say a few words."

I looked around quickly for a girl with one bare foot and plum-colored eyes. My father recognized the man. "Go ahead, Ben. Tell her to speak."

Ben nodded to his group and the small turbaned woman stepped forward. She stood there in her short black coat, her small feet in sensible black oxfords placed at parade rest, cropped gray hair looking as if a child had trimmed the edges with pinking shears.

"Comrade Jack. You were a loyal comrade. You will not be forgotten. We, your friends, will carry on the fight so that you will not have died in vain. You had no wife, no children, but you worked and risked your life so other men's children could live in a better world. We will never forget you." She stepped back in a military manner and rejoined her group.

I sensed the uneasy stirring around me. Faces, the ones I could see, still wore the mask the occasion required when Aunt Fannie said, "What a nerve! The way she made dirt of him, to come here now with her politics—"

My father, wiping his eyes, put a restraining hand on his sister's shoulder. "*Shah, shah.* Let him rest."

Semper Fidelis

Mrs. Chodash, in the 1700s court of the garden development that I've managed for the past few years, has gentlemen callers in the early afternoon. Not many, according to the two women who came in to complain and left their baby carriages parked under my office window, but isn't it a shame for the children, and if Mr. Chodash, the bald and burly Cascade Diaper man, would *shtup* her regularly, what's that I say, knock her up, the taller prow-bellied woman says, why she'd have plenty to do and our kids wouldn't ask embarrassing questions. I murmur something about can't legislate tenants' morality and then a vague I'll look into it.

Mr. Chodash slams into my office a few weeks later. He tells me openly he kicked the front door in when his wife didn't answer quickly enough, and he wants the door fixed and a new lock installed. I'll bill you, I say. And then he wags his forefinger almost in my face: any mother's son who fools around with my wife is going to feel this, and he balls his fingers into a heavy fist. I know he's strong enough and mad enough to hurt someone.

I got there quicker than the ambulance or the police, a few weeks after the door was fixed and the new lock installed. The tall neighbor lady, big enough to be carrying twins, told me Mr. Chodash came home early today. Bert had delivered the meat order an hour before (they know everyone's movements), and Bert had tried to slip out the bathroom window, had dropped from the second floor and broken his leg.

Mr. Chodash is cradling Bert's head on his lap, the gray Cascade Diaper jacket covers Bert's thin body, and Mrs. Chodash is standing over them, her hands clasped across her plump bosom in an attitude of silent devotion. She is wearing a long raincoat but it's not raining, and her bare feet indent the thick grass. Chodash bows his head and tears roll down his cheeks, splashing on recumbent Bert's white forehead. The ambulance rolls up and two men and a young girl jump out. They pull out a stretcher and quickly—

I told my wife, I fully expected them to pick up Mr. Chodash, not Bert.

She says, you wanted her yourself!

I'm astonished. Plump, red-dyed hair, Mrs. Chodash? So I answer perversely, remembering Mrs. Buchsbaum, sans Mr. B, bobbling toward me over the greensward, in tight white tennis shorts, a blue T-shirt, and jauntily swinging a tennis racket. I DID!

I don't want to sleep with other men. Have no desire to at all but you—

I admit it. I do.

What if I slept with someone else? How would you like that?

Don't risk it, please. I'd black your eyes and kick him in the nuts.

Well, I wouldn't. It's immoral.

It's not.

What's holding you back then—if you want to so badly—why did you ever get married?

Who knows? I'm happy married.

I'll bet you're sleeping around.

I'm not. Remember the rabbi who married us, how wide he opened his mouth, the gold-capped teeth, and I told you he should have had his adenoids removed when he was little, would improve his diction—I promised that wide-mouthed rabbi, I promised to be faithful to you, to us.

You're illogical!

No. A concordat is a concordat. It transcends morality.

You're a liar.

I'm not.

I can never tell when you're lying and when you're telling the truth.

I can, I say flatly. I kiss her but she keeps her clear eyes open wide. Very wide. In fact, she stares into mine. I begin to wonder when I lied and when I told the truth. I love you, I say to myself, testing the sound.

Almost any night, when I walk out of the railroad station I see the commuters' wives lined up waiting for their husbands. The men open the car doors on the driver's side and the wives slide over docilely. The men peck the wives on the cheek. The wives peck back.

We do better, my wife and I. I carefully tend the outside of our house and plant things in a mad riot of color. My wife lectures at the university. A few days, someone comes in and washes clothes and cleans. I train the children in outdoor maintenance and appreciation. My wife handles all their school subjects.

I only went as far as college algebra but I always take an interest in my wife's work and comment intelligently. Once she threw this one at me from her doctoral course: A Naive Approach to Set Theory. In a village there is a barber who shaves everyone except those who shave themselves—who shaves the barber? I puzzled a half-hour over that one. Later that afternoon I thrashed her 6-0 at tennis; always carried her to 6-3 or 6-4 before.

I sewed a button on my brown tweed sport jacket and a button on my navy-blue raincoat. I turn my business shirts into Mao shirts when they wear out. It's simple to do. Just tear off the collars and cut the sleeves at the shoulders and they become splendid gardening shirts. The other night, I sewed a button on the collar of my blue button-down shirt. Then I made out a list of easy upkeep shrubs: two *Hypericum* (yellow-flowering, also called St. Johnswort), three Potentilla, two smoke bushes (*Continus coggyria*), two glossy spicy sweet shrubs, and two Annabelle Hydrangea. I was writing the to Spring Hill Nurseries, Tipp City, Ohio 45366 for $28.73, when I sensed my wife standing over me. Where will you put all those things? she asked. I looked up at her and then looked out the rear window. Tulip bed, vegetable patch, iris and lily beds, annual area. I'll plant them in tiers, above the other stuff, I said. She stared at me. I tore up the check.

In the morning I yelled goodbye to my wife, heard the car pull away, and slipped into my blue button-down. The side where I had sewed the button curled up like an epaulette. I took it off, a good shirt too, and tore off the collar, cut the sleeves at the shoulder, and turned it into a Mao shirt, hanging it with the others. I quickly counted and this one made Mao shirt no. 13.

In the last few years, my friends' wives have begun kissing me, at first cautiously, then with wild abandon. My wife gets kissed by their husbands too. It's sad to see kissing depreciated this way (used to be confined to New Year's Eve or pretend-drunk party time), but I went along with it and kissed back perfunctorily like the others: on entering their homes, on leaving again, and once unexpectedly in the supermarket between the Pet Food row and the Sugar and Spices.

A Jewish political-activist wife (part-time dissector of dogfish in a college laboratory, who that night wore black net stockings and tight, shiny black rain boots) kissed me, and like Rudolph Valentino in a late-night TV flick, I embraced her, loved her, glued my lips to hers, bent her backwards, one hand around her waist until her platinum tresses touched the Scandinavian rya rug.

No one kisses me any longer.

A couple of weeks ago, in a store window on Christopher Street, I spied a hobby horse. A beautiful thing, all rosy-cheeked and ivory with a black panache of a tail, and I wanted it. I'd buy it and put it in the living room. The price tag—I craned my neck to see it, where the little horse hung high in the tall narrow window—read $23.96. I opened my wallet and counted twenty-seven dollars. I longed for that horse. I didn't know what I'd do with it. I could afford it. I have enough money to treat myself to a luxury. Yet I turned away without going into the store.

Now I'm back on Christopher Street and can't find the store. I try Charles Street, pass La Sevilla where I've eaten a couple of times, once with an earnest lady lawyer. The lady lawyer frightened me that evening. Remarkable woman. She completes my sentences while I'm just rumbling a portentous opening remark (my wife says she can die a lingering death waiting for me to finish a thought). She tugged her skirt down and excused herself to go to the john when I stared at her knees. I scared her too. Try Barrow Street, try a few more streets, come back to the same place as you always will in the West Village, an area I know, yet an area I always permit myself to get lost in, so I wind around, ah, there's the store, try the other side of Christopher Street, now I've traversed the entire length of it and can't find the store, can't find the hobby horse, and I tell myself, next time, next time, I find the horse, I'll buy it on the spot, come what may.

I had a crazy dream and it still worries me because I rarely dream, so any dream is a worry.

I awakened in our smoke-filled bedroom and my wife wasn't next to me where she belonged. Dashed out the door and shook my two older daughters awake, both heavy sleepers, and they tumbled downstairs, then got my son. My youngest daughter is in my arms. Carrying her half-asleep in one arm, I ran down the stairs and outside.

So far the dream is O.K.

Now I see. 20—BEAUTIFUL JEWISH HOUSEWIVES—20 all strolling around the front lawn, dressed in pastel-colored, form-fitting trousers; walking, not in any direction, just meandering. They walk, my paler wife among them, like married bridesmaids at a Jewish wedding, with a certain unmistakable arriviste tilt to their chins. My wife doesn't seem to recognize me. I met her on a windy picket line. Turned away from a fur-coated Antioch girl to warm my wife's shivering flesh. Now she's picketing me. What's her sign? What does she want? Higher wages? She's a professor. Shorter hours?

All the 20—BEAUTIFUL JEWISH HOUSEWIVES—20 are trampling and pummeling the grass with their bare feet. Legs very good, all around. Ages—can't tell, just not clear but sure they're over twenty-five and under forty. They undulate as they perambulate like sleepwalkers. I can't get their attention—they all look through me—too stupid to call the Fire Department—must I do everything—so I go around to the back of the house to find the kids. Two daughters and one son are sitting at the redwood picnic table playing Scrabble. My youngest daughter weighs heavily on my arm. I take a second look at her tousled head, and she's grown and aged five years, now about eight, I guess. Indifference all around me. I start to go back into the house, someone must call the fire depart-

ment: I'm driven back by the smoke and the flames. Where the hell
are the fire engines? I awaken and it's dark and I hear a radio playing loudly: *Cecelia, you're breaking my heart.* The sounds stop. An
empty silence. I lie there in the darkness and figure out the first part
of the dream easily. I stopped going to my psychiatrist two years ago,
when after the fifth visit he said, you're a very serious case. I think
you should begin coming twice a week. Yeah, yeah, Doc. But how
long? I asked. One month? Three months? Three years, at least, he
said, maybe longer, five or six years. I quit, Doc, I said. So ever since,
I practice psychiatry on myself. I wanted to fuck those 20 BEAUTI-
FUL JEWISH HOUSEWIVES, that's plain enough, and I saved $60
a week for five years or approximately $15,000. But the second part
of that dream, I just don't know, and I couldn't confide in my wife
about the first part or the second part so I'll just have to wait and
puzzle it out.

An ocean voyage to a foreign country, without children, even those
children one loves desperately and indispensably, gives one an
opportunity to figure things out.

All the guidebooks promised magnificent, ancient castles with
stone watch towers, battlements, and 48 centrally heated rooms.
When we arrived, the castles were all called Bunratty, Dunfarfel, or
Cuntfarfel. And if the Irish government had not turned the castle
into a restaurant where colleens served whole sheep washed down
with poteen and sang rump-pinching songs, then all that remained
were a few gray stones and the bare irregular outline of a foundation
wall in an overgrown field.

I sit at the gray plastic-topped table, elbow touching my wife's, in
the farthest corner of the dark workingmen's bar, surveying. Look at
the shiny black pants seat of the man learning against the bar,
properly capped like me. I get up and stand next to him. He's
nursing a pint of Guinness. Order a second Irish for me and a cream
sherry for my wife. I couldn't wait to get out of Dublin where a walk
along the dirty river Liffey meant meeting the beggar women carrying vacant-eyed, scabby-faced, and putty-fat babies. Here—take my
change—go away. The Times Square honkytonk of O'Connell
Street, an affront to the martyred brothers executed in the troubles.

And wherever I turned, the sinister laundry trucks, large swastikas boldly embossed on the trucks' white sides.

Why are you sitting like that, my wife says, all scrunched into the corner? And rolling your eyes that way? Expecting anyone?

Away from the windows, watch the entrance.

Oh?

Bogart sat this way. Also Kevin Barry, but they hanged him poor lad.

Nut. Happy nut. She drops her hand on my wrist.

If I were captured by the Black and Tans, and taken from our boardinghouse in the middle of the night, as they started to throw me into the truck, I'd holler, loud and clear—LONG LIVE THE REPUBLIC OF IRELAND. You'd run down the stairs in your nightie and grab my arm, trying to keep them from taking me. An English Tommy in a pie-shaped helmet is pulling on one arm, you're dragging on the other—now what do you say?

Leave my husband alone.

No.

He's Jewish. I'll call the embassy.

So was Mayor Briscoe of Dublin. No—

I give up.

LONG LIVE MY HUSBAND—that's what you should say.

But why should you get mixed up with the I.R.A.?

I might, or then again, I might not. But still you should say: Long Live My Husband.

Oh Ben. She reaches up to snatch my cap but I pull my head away.

As soon as she walks into our bedroom she says, I'm chilly, Ben. I put a larger coin into the meter. The switch on the side is up but no red glow lights up the coils. I turn the switch down. My wife's standing over me.

She bends over and her hand follows a cable from the heater. Crouching and then sliding parallel to the wall, she traces the cable behind a six-foot clothes closet on wheels. She finds a switch here and flicks it up. The heater glows.

Sit down, I say, grabbing her wrist, so she tips over and faces me on the floor. You're much more intelligent than I am.

I am more practical, she says.

How long have you known? I ask.

Oh, quite a while, she answers.

You're more intelligent than I am. I'll have to keep remembering that. It's no crime to be less intelligent, is it?

Cut it out, Ben. Everyone likes you. You're fun-loving, more worldly—

What's funny about me?

You kicked the tires of the plane at Kennedy and said, it's safe to take off.

That's funny? You remember when you urged the kids to give you a rest and take their English homework to me. Because I read more fiction. But those kids of ours said, everyone in turn, just the answer, Dad. Get to the answer. My son said it too. You laughed. Then we all laughed.

You are funny.

Maybe, maybe, but you're smarter. Give me a few days to get used to it. I wonder how you hid it from me? Now that I know, must try to get to like it. You're smarter than I am.

II

In the Republic of Ireland, in the town of Tralee, an olive-skinned Spanish mistress of the hunt, wearing a black bowler, dirty white blouse, and tight brown jodhpurs, offers each of us an apple. The Shetland ponies are led out of the barn and saddled. The Spaniard crunches her apple with stained yellow teeth. I crunch my apple in a harmony of crunching.

The Spanish mistress tips her hat back on her head. Her two blouse buttons are open. The edge of her dirty white bra crosses her dark full breasts. The Spaniard tightens the girth on my pony. She had said to my wife while dispensing apples, I'll get your man, he's a big one, a horse-sized pony. She doesn't acknowledge the difference between a man and a husband. Resting one hand on my knee, she lowers the stirrups with the other. I look straight ahead.

My wife said earlier, I don't want to ride on ponies. Isn't it enough to be touring on bicycles?

I said, you could shop for gifts.

She said, whither thou goest—

I think I looked pleased. I dressed to leave, and when I adjusted my cap I heard: that Sinn Fein cap makes you look like a New York Jewish cab driver.

Fine, I laughed. Get dressed. I'll wait outside.

The Spaniard follows a winding path through a dense forest. I follow the Spaniard and my wife follows me. Out onto the asphalt road, a fine rain is falling and we string out, hugging the side of the road, when a Gypsy van loaded with kids and bedding squeezes by. The Spaniard trots, I trot, my wife falls behind. The saddle turns into a split rail. The Spaniard canters across the road and waits stoically. I join her and wait for my wife. My pony sidles toward the Spaniard's and their haunches smack together.

The Spaniard turns up a narrow dirt path that climbs a hill. The saddle becomes a knife edge; the road steepens and twists and narrows to a four-foot width and disappears into the curling mist; the forest clears, the trees are scrubbier, then only gray rocks, and the ponies are picking their way along an outcropping that cantilevers into the fog. Shrouded in fog, I can't see the Spanish mistress ahead. I hear my wife call out, where are you, Ben? I trumpet back, Dolores says these ponies are very surefooted. Just relax, honey, I sing out. My echo rebounds, ax honey.

Back in our room, I feel as if a hot iron has been pressed against my backside. My wife asks me to get the bath plug from the landlady. When I return, she's kicked off her bluejeans, slips her hand in her underpants, and caressing her own bottom, she says, look at my fingers, dripping with blood.

I look at her fingertips, moist and faintly pink. I put both my arms around her, dangling the bath plug across her behind. Our duenna turned the gas heater on, I say, takes about fifteen minutes for the water to get hot. Why waste fifteen minutes?

Say something meaningful.

I love thee.

Why thee?

I'm loving thee Quakerly.

Fakerly? Sum it all up, she says. Sum it all up.

I can't.

Try.

We've had fifteen good years.

Sixteen—what else?

I can't. Can ruin everything with talk. I tighten my hold. She pulls her head back to look at me, piercing my brain. I shrug and kiss her hard. Right hand still encircling her waist, I lean over and sweep the bed cover off with my left.

Trot, canter, gallop.

I roll off.

You've had a balanced day, she says. Fresh air, exercise, a good meal—Ben, Ben, you never, at no time, did you want me to go pony trekking with you. Now you've lost all power of speech. You're the only man I know who can shrug while he's lying flat on his back.

I did want you with me. You're the only thirty-eight-year-old woman on the East Coast who'd take a bicycle trip across Ireland with me. I look down at her hip when I say this, sure that would please her, her hip once like a ripe luscious peach.

You're not interested in the inside of me. Just satisfied with the service and surfaces: the planes, curves, and angles. Tell a funny story, Ben. Make me laugh.

You're killing it all, with too much mouth.

A couple of months apart, Ben, would do us both a lot of good.

I'm sure she expects a joke. Or at least, let's talk it over. Or silence. I agree with you, I say. I'm not smiling. I've pole-axed her.

I don't miss her at first. I've got my son, she has our daughter, and the older two are in camp. We're toodling along the side roads into Gt. Barrington, the kid on his new three-speed bike, me on my old Raleigh one-speed, and he can make some of the Berkshire grades—gets hilly after Sheffield—that I have to walk. Robbie's my passport. Without him a forty-two-year-old dude like me would look dangerous to the women, alone on these isolated farms. So he goes in for water to refill our canteens and comes out with a couple of apples too. And he crunches his apple, saying, very nice lady, and I think he misses his mother but he doesn't mention her. Asks once when we'll get some mail, and I tell him not before Bennington, care of General Post Office. On a back road near Pittsfield, just a dirt track that we jounce over and it's getting me in the kidneys, he stops for water, and waving from the porch, invites me in. The woman inside has just baked some chocolate chip cookies. She's about my age, asks if I'm a writer. No, I answer, and she shows me her article on *The Life Cycle of the Swamp Cabbage* in a Vermont magazine while my son is contentedly sipping a glass of milk at the kitchen table. I did have something published recently, I say, in a professional journal, *Greenbelt Revisited: Cemeteries and Garbage Dumps—the Future Sites for Urban Housing.* My husband would enjoy meeting you, she says; he's in architecture at Harvard. What a handsome boy, she adds, lowering her voice.

I look for signs of a husband in the large, sunny kitchen: pipe, odd hats, *Field and Stream, Architectural Forum;* can't see any. Then I sniff for husband spoor; can't smell any. When she bends over to pour another glass of milk for my son I see the curve of her stomach, and she brushes her hair back with her wrist, an unintentional coquetry—it thumps me.

At high noon, a half-mile swim to the center of a tear-shaped lake, and back through the clear blue sweet-tasting water, then through the green clutching lake weeds, and underwater when I reach the first few bathers; scrape the pebbly bottom and surface; wave to my son poised on the raft, and I walk up the narrow beach onto the thick grass.

I pull a towel from under the bike carrier, and holding the two ends, draw the towel back and forth across my back. Rhythmically I strum my shoulder blades, then I rub my upper arm, half turn it, and enjoy kneading the coiling triceps, a useless muscle but there it is. Clean, shriven of my sins and reborn, I grasp my thigh, it's a cable; pound my middle with my open palm, lost the office flab. I look around for someone to admire me—and there they are.

Two Swedes are lying on the beach, one man between them. Two sisters, I guess, lissome and outstretched on their bellies. Two heads face me: one with short flaxen hair, the older, longer tawny hair stricken with clean white. The man lights two cigarettes as each woman rises on her elbow. I love Swedes; hope they're not Germans but I'm prepared to forgive them when I peer into the shadows below their sharp collarbones. Either one will do but I prefer the older. They stare at me openly. The younger woman puts on a pair of dark sunglasses, and the man between laughs and throws his arm over her lean back. He's staked out one woman.

I get up and stretch, turn around so they can see the back muscles that at that moment I could use, if there were any need, to get under a Shetland pony and lift it high in the air. My son's just dived off the raft again. I pick up my pipe and tobacco and walk toward the trio. The older woman says, to me? to the others? *Unserer leute* (a post-graduate Hitler *Mädchen*), but I ask this handsome fraulein for a match.

A few days later, on the outskirts of Bennington, the kid scoots ahead and I get tangled up with a big wooly dog that nips at my heels and then keeps cutting in front of my wheel until I have to get off and walk the bike until the dog escorts me out of his territory. After we find a tourist house and clean up, we stroll into town and I see a crowd forming a line along a wide-board urban renewal fence on the main street.

A heavy woman in a beige linen dress is holding a sign: BOY-COTT GRAPES. I give my son a few dollars, tell him to meet me in an hour, and decide to join the vigil. I take my place at the far end of the line and stand with the others facing the street. The sun feels good in the cool of the late afternoon. I look at my watch and only fifteen minutes have passed, forty-five still to go. A police car drives slowly past. I close my eyes, gaze at the red haze of my eyelids. I open them. The scene hasn't changed. A long row of quiet stores across the street. A few storekeepers are beginning to draw their window blinds. I see my son passing the stores. He ignores me. Ashamed? I wonder. Of MR. CLEAN—the wholesome Dad? He walks into one store and out again. Into another one, and he emerges clutching a paper bag in one hand. He carefully discards the bag in a trash can and stuffs the purchase into his back jeans pocket. I recall he wanted a small pocket flashlight so he wouldn't have to ask for mine on trips to the outhouse at night. The shadow has advanced to the middle of the street. I reach out to my son's lean back and square shoulders. Then it's over at last, and the long line of twenty-five women (I counted them) and a handful of men break ranks and mill about. They talk in small groups in hushed tones. The silence is still on us. The woman leader asks if I'm a teacher. She says it's very good of a stranger to join them.

Then I unexpectedly spy a friend, and we walk toward one another; it's the lady of the chocolate chip cookies. She arrived late, she says, and gives me a firm handclasp. She's wearing a modest light print dress, just below the knee, it wouldn't do in New York, and her figure is good New England home garden, unselfconsciously thicker in the middle than suburban tennis figures, a good functional bosom, strong shapely legs, and she's delighted to see me. You must come home with me, she says, you and Robbie. I'll throw the bikes in the station wagon, you can stay over, and I'll bring you back in the morning. Wonderfully warm and open, she touches my shoulder, I glimpse my wife and can't recall her face, and we search for my son, standing shoulder to shoulder at curbside. I can't remember exactly what I've said but she assumes we're coming.

Brushing shoulders now, she doesn't draw away. My kind of woman, open and intelligent. Instead of going to church, she joins a vigil. She's bound to respect my ideas. My son's a sound sleeper. I don't recall how many bedrooms in her place. Two maybe. I can get up and go for a drink. Swiss cheese. I like Swiss cheese at night. Or the bathroom, I might have to go. No pajamas with me. Just slip on my jeans. She comes out when she hears me, offers to make toast, coffee. Or pours sherry, bending toward me as she pours, wearing a nightgown, flannel because the nights are chilly. Voluptuous in a plain thick white gown, maybe a ruffle at the neck. Slip my hand up and under—no, she's not wearing pajamas—not that problem, slip the bottoms down from around her bounteous hips, my fingertips tingle, a bounty, pink rounded flanks—that's it—and I didn't meet her at the corner drugstore or a church supper, a chance meeting, it was fated, she came here—the vigil—knew I'd be here, because she knows me, wants to really know me, wants me back again, in her home, kitchen, bedroom, bed—then I hear, my husband will be up from Cambridge later tonight and he'd enjoy talking shop.

Husbands, husbands, I think, who needs more goddamned husbands? I'm one husband and she's a wife and that's enough. So I beg off with, I'll see you again, I'm sure at another vigil someplace, and hurry across the street. See my son walking quickly toward me, want to break into a run and grab him, hug him, but it would only embarrass both of us.

The following day I reroute the trips. Why go to Montreal? The Expo is over. And Quebec will always be there. So I begin circling lakes, my son doesn't care, and we circle Newfound Lake, Squam Lake, then south to swing around the western and along the southern end of Lake Winnipesaukee in easy stages, and then on to Conway, when suddenly I don't know why I'm circling lakes and I must get home. If I can get a Sunday bus, I can meet her train from Chicago on Monday.

On the bus I tried my friends' wives. The giantess, warm and willing, wouldn't do. And the sweet-faced one, thick-ankled and in such need, I ached for her once, no good either; and the dark callipygian divorcee, a cliché, whose every throaty breath called me, slipped away like an impossible dream—and further back: the stout-hearted union maid in the bar; me, three months married, and Ray Robinson is giving Jack LaMotta a terrible beating in the TV set over the bar; we're nursing two beers, the girl said all the best men are married, and I believed her and can't recall her face but remember her heaving need, the offering of heavy well-molded thighs and the terrible sincerity.

My wife walked right past me and my boy, on the Grand Central platform, unseeing. It was my daughter who spied me first, and I lifted her, although she's too big for it, and hugged her tightly, looking over my shoulder into my wife's dark eyes. Dark brown, they once were, I'm sure of it, but now they're eggplant black. Must be the enlarged pupils, in the dim light of the platform; all the other travelers seem to have rushed away.

Once home, the two kids fly out to visit friends. I embrace her, hold her tightly, drop my hands to the elastic at her waist, to her hips. She's unfamiliar under my hands, not my wife—she's every woman I've ever touched. We move apart, I've forgotten everything I wanted to tell her, and she busies her hands with the coffeepot. You scared me, Ben. You looked like Malcolm X on the platform.

He's not a bad fellow.

You've gotten thinner. I like you better a little heavier. When your cheeks are rounder, you look more boyish. What have you been eating?

Let's do it now.

You crazy old coot. The kids may be back any moment.

So let's do it in the bathroom, standing up. We'll lock the door.

You're nuts!

The Irish do it that way—

You're not Irish.

I've been very good. Only played with myself twice in six weeks— then I become ashamed, she's reduced me to pleading; and I spend the rest of the afternoon weeding savagely. Fill two garbage cans and three plastic bags, try to salvage the tomatoes, throw away the rotted ones, stake the plants that have fallen over, nip dead flower heads; start the lawn mower, it gets clogged in the high grass; take out the grass whip, my back aches, arms are falling off; start the lawn mower and mow and rake and weed until dark.

Our bedroom contains: one king-sized bed and three bookcases overflowing with mathematics texts. The bed is hollowed on my side. I sleep well this way, resist buying a new mattress, and sleep badly when the mattress is turned and the hollow is on my wife's side; then I'm on the plateau and my wife's in the valley.

The wall on the head side of our bed is painted dark hunter green: the other walls apple green. I'm in the hollow. A couple of drinks on our friends' place north of Albany and I take her hand and we wander into the furze. Lovely woodland scene. Cranberry viburnum with bright red fruit. I pull her along in an unsteady path. I fall down on her, my pants around my ankles, her bare ass on the earth.

I need a woman, I say, and you're my wife. I finger her, handle her, fondle her, in all the old ways, practiced ways.

You're a stranger, she dares tell me.

I run my tongue over her parched lips, between her teeth. I hoist her right leg and we're side saddle.

To Post! Walk. Trot. Canter.

Who am I, I say?

I can smell the smoke in your armpits, she says. Go on. Go on! Who am I?

Gallop along, my bucko, finish it all.

Who am I?

My husband. My husband.

I gallop off then. The usual, scalding, splitting stars.

You bastard, she says, matter-of-factly.

If she stiffened now and died, I'd get married again. It might be to the first woman I met when I walked out of the house in the morning. How do men live alone? Leave an empty bed to go to work, return to a womanless house at night, nothing alive next to them, pulsing. I rub my calf where she raked me with her long toenails. I always have to remind her to cut them and there's been no one to remind her for two months. No one face comes before me—no composite either—just a middle-sized woman, neither too fat nor too thin. A woman with all the proper appendages: breasts, legs, hair; no particular hair color. The woman is on the old side of young or gracefully touching early middle age. I ask her to marry me and she consents and off we go, arm in arm.

She's lying outstretched, both hands crossed over her breasts, unstirring.

Die! You daughter of the candy store, flaunting your father's 1934-5-6 relief checks, like a Red Flag, in my face.

I deserve cancer of the throat, rectum, and gonads for this.

Die, you stuffed cabbage–cooking, unliberated, brilliant, sexy, college-prof wife.

I deserve the electric chair for this.

Die, you doormat, you hard-working helpmate, you mother of my children.

For this: the gas chamber!

I've killed you at last. Thank God! I've killed you. I'M FREE. I'M FREE.

*Entrez/s'il-vous-plait/*On the Rue de la Paiz/Or the Place Pigalle. I wrote a poem that first night she went away. It's lying right in the top drawer of the night table, pinned down by a vaseline jar. I might have taken it out tonight and read it to her. It's not a very good poem but one line says: you're Marilyn and Ingrid and Mother Courage.

I turn toward her, touch the tips of my fingers gently to her thigh. She unfolds her hands and drapes both legs over mine; she always sleeps best this way. Now, I could never leave her. Never!

The Witness

I'm sipping tea and I hear my mother say softly, I met someone. I put the cup down, sloshing yellow into the white saucer, and she is staring at her cup as if she's reading her fortune in the tea leaves. Then she raises her eyes, staring into mine defiantly.

I take a good look at her. She has a flat Russian peasant face and full ruddy cheeks which I've inherited so she always looks as if she's just come in after a walk in the wind. She gets up and pours the rest of her tea into the sink and I hear: He came over while I was waiting in the bus terminal. Very polite and offered to buy me a coffee. She stands at the sink, back turned. A lot of older people sit on the benches, she says, and pretend they're waiting for a bus. I was really waiting.

I realize then that my own mother has straight legs and all of her friends, poor things, don't. And when she came to school during Open School Week, the teachers said you must be Phillip's mother. I'm made in her image. And later, a teacher said to me, your mother is a handsome woman. There had been a man or two I could remember, but my mother's too stiff, and nothing came of it.

Mom fills the green enamel coffeepot and that signals the end of my rare weekday visit. She sits down and slices two pieces from a nut-filled *bobka;* a one-inch slab for me and a sliver for herself. She fingers a pendant, a blue stone set in a dull white metal triangle, hanging from her neck. When I called you from the Brooklyn Museum last Saturday, Phillip, and said I couldn't visit this weekend, did I sound different? I shrug. Mr. Felsher bought this for me in the gift shop. He said: My city pension is $3,800 a year; my bankbook $4,500; my savings bonds $2,500, not cash value but maturity value. We'll put everything in both our names. We'll be one.

I lean forward: You just met him. Who is he? I didn't like my voice. Mom continues: Israel Felsher said, I'm sixty-seven; if you don't believe, I'll show you my birth certificate. Also, my high school equivalency.

You shouldn't rush into it, Fanny. You're not a heartsick. . . .

Phill-Up! I'm not asking for advice. We know each other four months. I knew my wife four years, I say. These are modern times, Philly, she answers unsmiling.

Before we get married, and do as Israel says, I want you to take this withdrawal slip and take $2,500 from my account, put it with your money, just keep it for me. She slides the slip across the table.

Nothing doing, I say, it's wrong. I take out my wallet and slide the green rent check toward her. It's early for the check, she says. Saves me a stamp, I say. Then I tear up the withdrawal slip, slowly, into four pieces, then eight. She pockets the rent check. I tear the slip into sixteenths, then find I can't tear sixteen pieces of withdrawal slip into thirty-two. She says if I had finished the typing course when Papa died, I could have been an office worker, maybe a bookkeeper instead of a finisher. I'm good at figures. She gets up to turn the jet off under the coffee and I begin tearing the sixteen pieces of withdrawal slip, piece by piece, until I have thirty-two tiny pieces. I sweep the pieces off the table, a few crumbs along with them, and drop them into my jacket pocket.

Mom got married a few weeks later, and I felt hurt that they didn't ask my wife and me to stand up for them as witnesses, at least. Instead, they asked two new friends they called the bus terminal couple—a pair who had known one another for two years and whom Mom and Mr. Felsher were urging to get married.

The newlyweds visit us and it's better than before when Mom came alone. Mr. Felsher brings gifts for everyone: pipe tobacco for me, candy for my wife, a dump truck for my three-year-old son, and a book for my six-year-old daughter. In no time, he's reading *The Bear Came over the Mountain* to both my kids, my boy is soon calling him Pop-Pop; and in the afternoon, the door never closes as the children's friends are invited in to meet the new grandpa.

I must admit Israel is a good-looking man, a few inches taller than my mother, thick black hair combed all the way back, only gray at the sides—I'm going bald early like my father—long-lobed ears that come to a point at the top and give him a devilish look. When he rolls his shirtsleeves up, I can see strong hardworking forearms covered with curly black hair.

How's married life, Fanny, I say to her, when I catch her alone in our kitchen. We walk in the morning, sometimes up Ocean Parkway or on the Boardwalk. Later, I may take a nap. I play cards with a few friends. He says go, go. I'm all right. Israel brings me library books —Sholem Asch and Stefan Zweig—other hard works. I think he wants me to be more intellectual. You're smart, Mom, I pat her shoulder. She says, I had to buy bifocal lenses and I can't finish all the books. My husband says Edna Ferber is trash. I never call him Izzy. They call I. F. Stone Izzy, Mom. Yes, she says, but not Mr. Felsher.

My mother returns to the living room and sits looking out the window at my kids building a snowman. I see Israel take her sweater from the couch, place it around her shoulders, and squeeze both her arms.

I visit a few weeks later; the elevator creaks its way up and expires on the sixth floor. Israel greets me with a strong handclasp. Your mother's visiting a neighbor, he says. He takes the green enamel coffeepot and fills it, measuring coffee carefully. I hope your mother is as happy as I am. She's opened her heart to me. I'm the wanderer in Dostoevski's *White Nights*—that *schlimazel* had three meetings with his beloved and lost her on the fourth night. Lucky me, we have many more years.

I look around while he's fussing. Two sets of red-bound books have been added to the maple bookcase: Charles Dickens and Mark Twain, interlopers, above my old Books of Knowledge that I had refused to take when I moved out. To the right of the books, a new picture, the revolutionary army of Diego Rivera marches, guns on shoulders, and nearby Millet's *The Gleaners,* biblical women stooping to gather grain in an amber field. The picture doesn't quite cover the outline of my mother's old one. I strain to recall it but can't remember. My new father is bombarding my mother with culture. Now Fanny is no marcelled sixty-year-old with a svelte figure like my friend's mother who admires Eldridge Cleaver, but Mom can hold her own. She's a good listener, and when I told her in 1948 that Henry Wallace was the man for President—I was fifteen then—she voted Truman although I didn't find out until years later.

I don't expect you to call me Pop-Pop, I hear, but you should know who I am. Israel goes into the bedroom and comes out carrying a large scrapbook. He sits, resting the book on his knees. A housepainter, he says, has lots of time to think. The brush paints by itself after so many years. So I composed letters to the editor. At night when I got home, I'd write them out. Letters here, he taps the book, to the old *New York World* and *World-Telegram* and *PM* and the *New York Post.* I've never made the *Times,* he says regretfully, but I keep trying.

I reach for the book and open it. The dates and newspapers' names are printed in heavy black marking pencil and each letter is pasted neatly in the middle of a single page.

I leaf the pages: letters on Dangerous Sidewalks, Police Sleeping on Post, Loud Fire Sirens, End the War. One letter catches my eye so I stop to read aloud. Dispel the powers of darkness in the Criminal Courts at 100 Center Street! How can the defendant, caught, pilloried, and then jailed by the awesome power of the law, keep up his spirits in the dingy, dark corridors of the Criminal Courts. I urge you, Mr. Mayor, to repaint the walls in a light, cheerful color and install new lights!

I look up and say: Let there be light.

Israel, eyes shining, replies, and there was light. Paint too. Six months later, the lobby, the courtrooms, everything redone and bright. *Bright!* I hear returning footsteps in the hall and Israel retrieves the book, almost snatching it away, and walks quickly into the bedroom.

The months slip by, my mother seemingly contented and praising her new husband, how helpful he is, how generous. Israel tells more: how just before he met my mother he led a group of senior citizens to Washington to lobby for higher social security payments.

One day, at our house, the children asleep, my mother and wife at the movies, and I·mean to ask Israel about his afternoon walks. Mom had mentioned that after their walk on the Boardwalk in the morning and lunch, Israel left again and didn't return home until supper. I said: Why don't you ask him? It's hard, she answered, I don't like to snoop. Mom used to plague me with the usual Don'ts— Aaron's mother called, don't drag him on the garage roofs. You'll break an arm. So I'd climb from garage roof to fence to tree to the next garage roof and tear my pants. Where did you tear those pants? Playing football, I said. She'd go back to reading the *New York Post.* A reasonable lie was always acceptable. She had done her duty and warned me. I did what I had to do. An excellent modus vivendi, now that I think back on it.

I give Israel a cognac and sit back sipping mine. I find myself hypnotized as he begins to talk like an Old World rabbi who has taken elocution lessons in English.

Did you know, Phillip, that in the old days, the brave ones who booed and hissed in a theater in Odessa when the audience chanted God Bless the Czar, that these men were sent to Siberia. I know, I murmur, and then he goes on; they shaved half their heads, tied a chain around the waist, and from this chain belted two heavy chains to the ankles. And you, Israel, I say, you wrote a letter to the *Petrograd Times* and they published it and—Don't fool around, Phillip, I was too young. But when I came here and I was just a young squirt, I stood in Union Square listening to a speaker, maybe a Socialist or a Communist, does it matter, and the police came and pulled him down, and I said let him speak and they took me to the station house and I won't lie to you and tell you they locked me up for a week, no, they released me the next day, just shoved me out with the tip of a club between the shoulder blades. He grows silent.

I'll adopt you, Israel. Every boy needs a father.

He gazes into space as if he has not heard my magnificent offer. I wonder, he says, his hands braced on both knees, what it would be like to be in jail for a week, a month, a year. Then he reaches for the cognac and drains it in one gulp. I forget to ask about his mysterious walks.

A few weeks later, I phone my mother. Her voice is very stiff. What's wrong, Mom? Nothing, she says. You're lying, Mom. Exactly like the time you made me get rid of my dog and said its fur was giving Pop asthma attacks. I'm not lying, she says. I'm not saying. All right and I slam the phone down and then pick it up again but just hear the humming.

After a half-hour passes, I dial again. The phone rings a long while and I count eleven, twelve, thirteen rings, when Mom finally gets on and says, who is it? Red Ryder, I say. How many gentlemen callers do you have? Who is it! Who else can it be but your devoted only son Phil. Now what's wrong, Fanny? Level with me. She says, Israel left all day, came back after midnight and didn't say where he was. Ask him, Mom, just ask him. He should tell me without asking, I hear. Should I come over? No! I stare into silence. I want to yell, Fanny, Fanny—cry—laugh. Tell me my children are beautiful. Praise my wife, my house. Why do our few remaining relatives sit embalmed, looking like the occupants of the first pew of the Congregational church? And one of these corpses told me at a funeral, our family get-together, he told me you were engaged to be married, left almost at the altar, and married my father on the rebound. What games did you play as a little girl? You're robbing me. Where did we come from? We're Jews, Fanny. I love Jews because they cry. Cry with me. I'm coming over, I say. Tonight! No, she says again and just as firmly.

The phone rings, an instrument of torture, but I rush to pick it up.

Israel: She won't talk to me.

Me: Tell her about your travels.

Israel: I can't, Phillip.

I'll torture Israel with my silence.

Israel: You adopted me, Phillip, remember?

Me: What can I do?

Israel: You come over. She must talk again. Any kind of talk.

Me: She was never a great talker. You're the talker.

Israel: Yes, but the silence was friendly. Not any more.

Me: I'm coming. In one hour, maybe sooner.

When I pull up to my mother's building, Israel steps out of the entrance door, hurries over, and wrenches the car door open. He grasps my elbow and turns me toward the Boardwalk. He walks briskly down the street and I follow a half-step behind. The Eiffel Tower of the parachute jump reaches into the dark purple sky, then disappears behind the new apartment building on Surf Avenue. As we walk up the Boardwalk ramp and turn right, the mercury vapor lamps go on. The unpeopled Boardwalk becomes pocked by luminescent green cones. Israel skirts the first pale green shadow and I wait for him to speak. He slows down and now we are strolling past the closed-down, sheet-metaled concessions: Dodge-Em Cars and Frozen Custard and Games of Chance.

I missed the 5:30 bus in Camden, he says. Then I walked around town; a cesspool. I couldn't even find a newspaper. I got home after midnight. Fanny didn't say a word, not one word. She stared at me, went into our bedroom, and shut the door. Why didn't she ask: Where have you been, Israel?

Where were you?

The Camden 28 trial. You heard about it, Phillip, the defendants broke into desks and file cabinets and poured ketchup over the draft records.

They didn't mention your name in yesterday's paper, Israel. And what were you doing there?

He stops and faces me. Doing! *Doing!* I defend along with them. I leap into the jury's minds. I wrestle with them. I defend. The jurors heard me. *Not guilty!*

Fine, Fine. I'm really glad. I rest my hand on his shoulder. Why didn't you tell Fanny the whole story? I see the lights of the apartment buildings to my right. The surf rumbles softly and the sea air smells as I have always remembered.

My wife—your mother—Israel speaks haltingly now; he has lost his fervor. She is a simple woman and just wouldn't understand.

How wrong you are, Israel! Do you know that Fanny joined a

strike against higher meat prices? Didn't she ever tell you? And it was her idea that saved the strike. The women were reluctant to picket their own butchers and Fanny proposed that the ladies change assignments and picket butcher stores where they were not customers.

Really, really? He grabs my shoulders and shakes me. You're telling the truth? You're not lying?

The truth. The truth. Now tell me where you were the other afternoons when you didn't come home until suppertime.

I go to trials. The Criminal Court is the best but sometimes I go to Landlord and Tenants Court for a change.

Take Fanny next time. She'll pack a lunch. Why do you go?

I bear witness. Always for the defendant.

You never thought they might, Israel, just might be guilty?
Never!

And in all the other trials, was a defendant ever found guilty?

Found guilty? Yes, of course. Sometimes they were judged guilty.

At that moment, I thought about Eichmann.

Israel says, the defendants are never guilty. I bear witness.

Israel, Israel, I chant. Down I squat, hands across my chest, like a Cossack; out goes one leg and fold it under, out goes the other, and I've caught the rhythm and my heels drum on the boards. I leap up, bound into the sky, and land in front of Israel with a thrust and stamp of both feet. Down I go, and Israel joins me, and his feet shoot out and back and legs flying we move together, brush shoulders and prance back. I stand up panting and Israel whirls top-like, his black hair flies into his eyes, and he circles completely around me and stands up, facing me. He takes one deeply drawn breath, overbalances to his left, and then straightens. Silently he searches my face. What is he waiting for?

Useless to invoke Jehovah, the angry one. I look up into the void. Can I expect some modest sign, a shooting star, anything? Israel is a lunatic. But since my mother and I have led such ordinary lives, this Israel, who is inflicted on us, must be an ordinary lunatic. God can't deal with ordinary cases—nothing to dig his teeth into. So it's back to us.

I turn away and begin to walk faster and faster, the zigzag walk, but I can't shake Israel. He hangs in there. So I tell him, let's go home now, she's waiting, and he smiles for the first time but remains silent, brooding over his next case perhaps.

The View from the
High-Sided Bed

A hospital is a very sexy place. Acres of bodies, clothed only in night-gowns that tie in the back with flimsy strings. When Farber walks to the bathroom, he must hold the back of the gown with one hand or it will fly open, exposing him. He wonders how the nurses and other workers can bear it. Why don't they throw themselves on those naked bodies in sounder condition, kissing, fondling private parts, sucking, penetrating the various orifices of the needy patients. It's an unequal world, the hospital: the bodies, white and black of various dimensions, lie there, all partly damaged; they lie there to be succored by the strong healthy meat of the nurses. The nurses wear frilled petticoats under their short white dresses and bend over, exposing the backs of heavy white thighs. How are you today, they chorus, and leave before you can muster a reply. A charm school for young girls, Farber muses. No modesty from these frisky nurses who dangle succulent breasts in his face.

In the hospital, Farber finds all his apertures under attack from the moment he gets into bed. The mouth cannot be defended at all; it receives green and white pills, red and white slippery capsules, flat discs, assorted junk. His penis, he is certain, will soon succumb to the invasion of the long gray catheter; and his asshole—on the third day (after two days of mouth temperatures), the baby-faced nurse with the passionless eyes comes in, draws the yellow curtain around his bed, and says, rectal temperatures are more accurate.

He rolls over, all witticisms failing him. She is extremely clumsy inserting the thermometer; first it jams against his spine, then it slips in, a cold alien thing, another opening breached; it becomes part of him, warm and surrounded and he embraces it. Farber tries to envision their roles reversed as he squints up toward her. She waits impatiently, her whole, strong, tight body bursting with milk and honey, but his imagination deserts him. He cannot utter one word. Nor can he imagine she would submit to having her temperature taken, ever, by him—even in fun.

Farber, who stopped smoking at the first announcement of cancer-connected pleasure and who favored regular exercise and moderate eating, landed in the hospital after the healthiest vacation he had ever assembled.

He had a premonition when he read the plaque on the wall of the Pinkham Notch Hut listing the thirty-seven persons who had died climbing Mt. Washington. He guessed one was definitely Jewish, a lawyer—heart attack—and two others possibly Jewish. These statistics did not overwhelm him until he sat hunched over a cup of coffee, eavesdropping on two couples, the men in their mid-twenties, Jewish boys from New York who had emigrated to school in Boston and taken up with two sisters, both scabby-kneed, strong-legged field-hockey players. Their conversation teemed with crevasse, pitons, handholds, sheer face, double belay, all dangerous talk. Farber feared for the young men's health. Dark handsome Jews with moustaches who could be safe in the Museum of Modern Art sculpture garden, climbing dangerous mountain passes and fucking the heathenish field-hockey players on moss-covered rocks that balanced precariously over a precipice. Farber, on the other hand, had planned a moderately difficult, solitary fiftieth birthday climb, not over treacherous windswept Mt. Washington but up nearby Mt. Madison.

While Richard Burton, on location in Africa, calls Liz Taylor in Monaco, Farber calls his own wife, complaining, the hospital pajamas don't fit or they're out of them and they bring me drafty nightgowns instead. Mrs. Farber brings a cornucopia of night wear: one yellow, shorty pajamas, one long blue pair with red piping, and one madras bathrobe with a long rolled collar. Farber protests

(out of years of wearing drawers or T-shirts or nothing to bed),
you're readying me for a lifetime of invalidism. Who needs all these
pajamas?

The second letter on her nameplate is blurred, the entire name
written in Old World script, so Farber never discovers if her name is
Marcy or Mercy Feigenbaum. She seems pleased when he calls her
the Pulmonary Nightingale for her habit of humming under her
breath when she adjusts the machine. She wears white slacks the
first day, and through the slacks when she bends over he can see the
checkerboard red and white of her briefs, very high across the buttocks and tight elastic around her thighs. She adjusts the Bennett
Pressure Breathing Therapy Unit, teaches him how to breathe in
and out evenly into the mouthpiece, and then hangs a sign OXY-
GEN IN USE—NO SMOKING on the door. Farber can't believe in
Mercy-Marcy. He fights against saying, you don't look Jewish; he
knows better: there is no classic Jewish look. She has a button nose,
broad forehead, taffy hair, a cleft in a strong square chin, a faint
second chin he also admires. A middleweight with the graceful
moves of a lightweight. She's not young, Farber coughs appreciative-
ly, nor too old, and he coughs harder from the innermost bronchi;
she smiles approvingly because that's her job, to make him cough up
his bad blood.

The third day she wears a tight white dress. She leaves him puffing
into the machine, walks to the door, hangs a DO NOT DISTURB
sign on the outside knob, then closes the door firmly. She returns to
the bed and, with solicitous fingers, tucks his balls into his short yellow pajamas. She draws the curtains around the bed, slips off his
shorty pajama bottoms, and squirting back-rub oil into her left
palm, inflates him with a few deft hand movements. Pressing the bed
button, she drops the bed to an almost horizontal position. She removes his glasses and carefully places them on the night stand.

She straddles him and all he can see is the rumpled white skirt
around her waist. As she raises the skirt higher, he fixes on her wink-
ing, palpitating belly button; his knees hurt and his neck too, he
can't continue holding it upright; she moves forward, hoists and
drops herself around him, bouncing professionally but poker-faced,

her nameplate a blur before his eyes. He finishes. She finishes. He is
sweating heavily.

When she releases him, he sees the concentration camp emblem
on her inner thigh. She says, don't think I do this for everyone. Only
for Jewish men, Mr. Farber.

Later, too tired to raise his head, he looks between the bed's bars
at the corridor filling with tall white legs. They hurry up and back,
past his door. Back and forth, the legs parade.

A white-stockinged leg, full and well-shaped, edges his door shut.
But the door stops a few inches from the jamb. Through the narrow
slit, he can see another door being shut across the corridor. Legs
wheel a covered body past the door. For two nights the body had
mewled. Once Farber had looked in. An old man who reminded him
of Iron Tail, the old Sioux, on the backside of the buffalo-head
nickel. A long nose, pale thin lips, unseeing eyes, but no dignified
Indian keening—a baby crying. Farber coughs into a tissue and
looks for signs of blood.

Farber's wife walks into hospital room no. 252, sits near the bed
on the molded yellow styrofoam chair, and the first words out of her
mouth are:

What's that blood spot on the sheet?

Loose lips sink ships, says Farber.

What's that blood?

Avec, avec, damned spot, Farber says.

What's it from?

Just before you arrived, I screwed a forty-five-year-old virgin. She
was very grateful. She didn't know she was a virgin.

I'm so lonesome. I hate to sleep alone.

Speechless, he stretches toward her and pats her dark brown hair.

After she leaves, Farber concentrates on the silent television set he
had refused to hire for three dollars a day, hanging high on the wall
in front of his bed. To the left, near the window, stands the beige
metal recessed cabinet that contains his street clothes (once he puts
them on and hikes again, he'll be whole), then he looks out the window at a few vagrant stars, and he recalls the careful trip that led
him here.

Puffed up with boundless health, he charged up the last 500 feet, displacing a rock that clattered down the mountainside. The spruce trees had turned wizened and twisted like a bonsai forest, the wind cut his chest, a long rocky slope fell away to the left, one more turn, only the red bunchberries remained hugging the bank on his right; gone, the dwarf white birch of the lower slopes; twenty more breath-robbing steps and he burst onto a rocky plateau. The Madison Hut stood alone, surrounded by interlocking stone fences that led to the hut door. On the bare plateau, unknown tiny white and purple flowers, green patches of mountain sandwort, finger-sized whorls of rough evergreen carpet. Cairns of rock led to a clear pool of water. Farber stood on the crater of the moon, above the tree line, and the wind pushed against his chest; he opposed it and leaned into it and walked through the rock-strewn maze to the hut entrance.

At suppertime, the hut boys crashed the dessert dishes onto the end of the table. A blond little girl took charge, and slid the dishes across the long tabletop. The ex field-hockey player across from Farber explained, only the blonde child was hers and the two dark children were his and she gestured with her index finger upraised toward the Talmudic bridegroom next to her. He stroked his wispy black beard, placed one finger of his other hand in the paperback he was reading, and swayed forward and back two or three times, nodding agreeably. He reopened his book.

Farber tried to pick out the two counselors and their eight reform-school honor students from Manchester who were being rehabilitated on the mountaintop. A deafening din from the thirty campers from a valley camp. While Farber poured coffee for his end of the table, the door opened and a woman in almost new denim shorts and soiled white T-shirt clumped into the room; on her feet, nine-inch boots, on her back, the heaviest, highest pack he had ever seen. She dropped her burden near the door, searched for an empty seat, then, walking with a deliberate attempt at lightfootedness, passed the first bench and stopped near Farber, standing before the empty place. The seven diners scrambled up and moved the bench so she could get to her chosen seat.

Where did you come from, he said, after she had settled in.

Lake o' the Clouds, she said, picking at her cold food.

That's quite a distance, alone.

It was my last chance, or close to it, and I wanted to do it, and I did it, and I feel very good.

He wondered at her enormous pack, too-high boots, the reddish-brown hair graying at the roots, the two cords, like taut violin strings, running from collarbone to chin. Pleading fatigue, she slipped into the women's bunkroom after supper.

Forty men and boys twisting and snoring in four-decker bunks, and a whistling wind that arose at 4:00 A.M. by Farber's watch forced him out of bed. He hadn't removed pants or flannel shirt, so he added a sweater and his windbreaker, pulled on his boots, and throwing a blanket over his shoulders, walked into the dining room. He stumbled over a bench in the darkness, then sat down, lit a bit of candle, warmed the bottom to drip wax into a small dish, and stuck the candle into the wax. Tried to read a paperback mystery while he leaned back against the drafty wooden wall, soles flat on the bench, book resting on his thighs to catch the candlelight; it was almost half past four, the large many-paned window reflected many flickering candles. Yesterday's late arrival opened the door from the women's sleeping quarters and walked in, on the balls of her feet, in the nine-inch boots.

He looked up from his book as she sat down near his raised legs. You've got guts to hike these trails alone, he said. Do you do a lot of hiking back home?

No. I never hike. On my feet a lot. She got up, leaned over Farber and lit a cigarette from the candle, did a little turn and sat again. I'm an inner-city nurse and walk all day. It's 180 steps from the elevator to the end of my wing. My husband stopped smoking and blew up to 260 pounds. He's gotten kind of lazy in many ways. Now he's at Lake Winnipesaukee racing his sailboat. I felt this was my last chance to do something I've always wanted to do and I rented the equipment and here I am.

You're amazing. I'm finding it hard going myself.

Oh, I can see you're in great shape. Probably not having a bit of trouble. Not at all like my husband, who, and I know I can speak frankly to you, has gotten neglectful in many ways.

A nurse enters the dark room and silently leaves a paper cup with pills next to his bedside.

Farber went bounding down the trail. They had started early and no one else seemed to be taking the Airline trail back. The trees grew larger, gathered strength, as the trail followed a series of switchbacks, past the stream from which he had drunk yesterday, into a full-sized spruce forest mixed with balsam fir. Down he went, sliding over loose scree, inner-city nurse bouncing along behind him. He followed the edge of a ravine, the stream winding far below. Now he came to a series of wooden steps, railroad ties, braced to aid the descent, a few silver maples here, and he stopped at the bottom for a step-rock crossing of a brook; the inner-city nurse pulled up, bumping her pack against his. She said, I've just got to stop and pee. Hold up a minute. She scrambled off the trail, slid her pack behind a rock, and pushed farther into the low-branched spruce undergrowth. He turned his back, heard her call out, mustn't be ashamed of the body's natural functions. I'm not. We nurses are used to everything.

Later, he was surprised when she refused to take off her boots, stopping him as he started to unlace her left boot. Dressed in shirttails, he mounted her. He scraped his knuckles trying to support her under him. A few quick movements and she came. She stiffened like a cheese board and lay back, pulling away from him, and while he leaned on one elbow, sweat chilling the small of his back, she became very businesslike, confiscated his drawers, turned away for a moment, and slipped the underwear between her legs, squeezing his precious gism into it. This seemed like cavalier treatment; his wife always popped out of bed and took a shower.

I needed this experience, she said.

So did I, he replied.

Mind if we hurry back? She glanced at her watch. I promised to call my husband before 1 o'clock so he can pick me up. She jumped up, pulled her jeans belt a little tighter. I'll just wash out these drawers for you. And then you will be ready, won't you?

Too lazy to hunt for dry underwear in his pack, he pulled on his jeans, and while he was tying his shoelaces a few drops sprinkled on his neck. Inner-city nurse stood over him, twisting the water out of his underwear.

He stood up, threw on his pack. Tightened the two shoulder straps, tightened the waist strap, tightened his jeans belt and the pants encased him, held his sex, underwearless, in some fond strange embrace. She hurried back to the trail and he followed, the wet underwear draped on the rear of his pack. She turned several times to look at him, silently entreating Farber to walk faster. He trudged downhill carefully, step after step, occasionally sucking on his scraped knuckles.

Here's your lollipop, don't swallow it, and Farber opens his eyes, accepts the thermometer under his tongue, and sleepy-eyed, watches the aide's blue, rolling, no-nonsense buttocks walk through the door. He switches on the radio:

Manson's girl friend held on $1,000,000 bail, 1,000 persons reported dead in earthquake in eastern Turkey, and the announcer's serious voice turns skeptical, Liz Taylor takes Richard Burton back.

What's the point to that, Farber says to himself. Liz, down where it counts: she smells bad! And as for Burton, his scrotum is covered with white hair. She's had face-lifting, diets, personal appearances wearing a black veil in the women's segregated section of the synagogue, and sex—so much private and public sex that she can't take it anymore—it bores her. Now she wants Burton and he wants her!

The Pulmonary Lady arrives early, before breakfast. When she busies herself cleaning the mouthpiece, he grabs her backside. He squeezes but his fingers meet armor plate. Gone, the gently curved buttocks in tight cotton skirt or white stretch jumpsuit. So he searches lower (she goes on with her work, ignoring him), until he passes the edge of the unexpected girdle and greedily fastens his fingers around her blood-coursing thigh. He hangs on. The thigh, with long streaks of fat running through it, turns crimson under his clutching fingers.

She pushes his hand away. Stop it or I'll report you to the head nurse!

How about my treat? he says plaintively.

No, not today. I looked at your chart. Your fever is too high.

Burton calls Liz from the African veldt-schmerz. Liz's maid answers; gone, Mr. Burton, she's gone to Switzerland. Not discouraged, Farber says, remember, Mrs. Farber, the day I bought you that copper bauble. He brushes it on the way by and slips his hand inside her blouse, cupping her right tit. He glissades the nipple with his palm, gratified when it rises for him. Her breasts are not melon-shaped as Gentile scriveners are wont to describe Jewish breasts.

Stop it, his wife says, glancing at the open doorway. How are you feeling today?

The same. He lets his other hand fall on her crotch where her legs are crossed and tries to slide his fingers between her tightly clenched, parsimonious thighs.

Then she kisses him on the forehead, breaks away and stands, adjusting her blouse and positioning the ornament equidistant between both lemon-sized breasts. Farber throws his legs off the bed, stands, and urging her, almost drags her by one elbow toward the bathroom but she pulls away easily. He goes into the bathroom and calls goodbye through the closed door. He listens for footsteps, ear to the door. He calls out, visiting hours are from 7:30 to 8:30, yet lots of people come at 7:15 and are let in.

She says, oh, now you want me to feel guilty for coming late.

He says, you've overstayed your visit now. LEAVE! He points to the closed bathroom door as if she can see his dismissing finger.

After he hears her retreating steps, he goes to work on his sex with both hands, tickling it, soaping, using one hand after the other in a steady rhythm, never missing a beat. It hangs flaccid and useless. So he tries the back-rub lotion, oils and greases it and strokes again with steady wishful strokes. Then longer, yanking, angry strokes. It grows but hangs there rubbery and confused—a false friend.

Farber returns to bed exhausted. Presses the bed levers. The back flies up, then down. He raises the foot of the bed. Down with the foot and the entire bed levitates, two feet higher than normal. He repeats the bed's maneuver but faster. Up, down, up, down—faster yet. Finished, done in, done for; he lies back and grasps the high white bar with his left hand.

One morning Mrs. Farber brings fresh clothes. He is going home. Farber puts on his socks, noting the toenails which he always loathed cutting are unusually long. So long that they might tear his new socks. New underwear, freshly pressed bluejeans, new sport shirt from which Mrs. Farber extracts the pins. Wheeled through the corridor by a candy-striper, on the way to the elevator, Farber casually glances at a woman's backside. Why, Burton, why? Burton, Burton, stop fucking Liz. Leave her tired body alone. Play King Richard the Second, play better King Lear. Knock it off, Burton— act your age.

Farber, in pajamas and slippers and an old coat sweater, lies back in a lawn chair enjoying the early-morning September sun. He rests his right hand on the silky head of Sandy, the golden retriever bitch, lying at his side, while with his left hand he turns the pages of the *New York Times*. He reads: Burton sends Liz the world's third largest diamond, having already given the largest. Liz sends Burton in Bechuanaland a Frankfurter wagon, complete with thirty-inch wheels, eight-rib blue-and-orange umbrella, plus thirty dozen franks and 260 cans of soda. Why these elaborate gifts? They'll soon be re-united and then it's Donner and Blitzen.

The sun shines full on Farber. He gropes in his coat sweater pocket for matches, an old habit, and his index finger enters the old pipe-burn hole and wiggles through the hole to the open air. Too hot to sit here. Into the house, and he climbs the stairs to his bedroom, Sandy pattering after him. Mrs. Farber calls through the partly ajar bathroom door, Hon, I'm borrowing your razor—

O.K., O.K. Glad you told me so I can change the blade when you're done. Very considerate.

The odor of myrrh and frankincense, lemon bath salts, underarm hair, Pathmark shaving cream, shaven legs, steaming pussy, curls under and around the bathroom door, assailing Farber's smeller. He tears himself away, gets on a chair, and in the back of his closet, be-hind an orange daypack, he pulls out the six forbidden pipes in their walnut rack. He fondles the bottom of his favorite bulldog pipe. Smooth, his fingers and palm ache for it and he cups it in his hand, brings the bowl to his nose—a stench. He replaces the pipes in their hiding place and decides to get dressed. When he removes his pajama bottoms Sandy nuzzles him, and although Farber had always shoved her away, this time he permits her to lave his testicles with her rough tongue. The dog licks and licks until her lust for salt is satisfied. Farber sprays his boots with silicone waterproofing. The dog snarls at the spray can in his hand and runs downstairs. Farber, sitting on the edge of the bed, yells toward the bathroom, it's time for a hike, wife. Get dressed. Let's take a walk like the old days.

In the forest pasionaria: on the day the pink berries peer between the striped leaves of Solomon's seal, and in the wetter, trail-side places the orange horns of trembling jewelweed mingle with the shorter blue dayflowers; on the day the early green acorns are crushed underfoot by the two walkers, crushed too the green and brown shards of broken beer bottles; on that day the touch of his wife's skin, touched many times before, absentmindedly or observing certain touching amenities, on that day her skin turns to fresh creamery butter and Farber (still shaky on his feet) joyously accepts this gift.

The Cavalryman

Two days late, at the end of the camping trip, the ranger finally found me and handed over my oldest sister's message. "Father had heart attack. Come right home. Love, Muriel." The ranger gave me a lift in his jeep to park headquarters; from there a fisherman driving out of the Adirondacks preserve took me to Utica, where I grabbed the first bus home.

As the bus settled into its steady run on the Thruway, I rested my head back, closed my eyes, and thought about my father. After a while I could almost smell the grainy earth smell in the back of his truck. I lay on the old mattress in back of the old man's Reo. We were all going shopping in the West End, Boston's Jewish section—the old man driving, Mama next to him, Muriel and Gladys squeezed into the cab, me half asleep. Gladys might join me later in the back and I'd burrow my head into her stomach, both of us cozy and warm under the scratchy brown blanket.

I loved the house in Auburndale. In winter I belly-whopped down the driveway on my new Flexible Flyer. Kerosene lamps and a black coal stove filled the kitchen with soft light and burning, live heat. In spring, huge lavender and white flowering lilac hedges lined the driveway going up the hill to the greenhouses. Later, the raspberry and gooseberry bushes gave red and dark purple fruit. I picked, and my mother made jellies in large pots on the stove while the peach kitchen walls wept condensation.

When you enter the living room, my great-grandfather, the cavalryman, stares at you with his round black eyes. A painting by a lousy Russian artist. Brass-buttoned gray uniform. Pressing against the tunic, a taut belly that starts at his chest and ends at his crotch. His right hand on a saber hanging at his side. Standing near a giant potted palm, he looks too big to sit on any horse I've ever seen. I imagine the uniform, kept in a brass-bound trunk and pulled out for the sittings, thirty years after the cavalryman had ridden a horse.

Just because my great-grandfather was in the cavalry in the Crimean War, Max, my father, could do anything. And he did. He named me Bennett. What kind of a name is that with Cohen tagging along after it?

I'm the American dream of Max's old age. He was over fifty when I arrived. Seven years after my sister.

I can't remember Max ever tired. When I worked with him, I couldn't be tired or hungry or thirsty either. And he was never sick, except for a cold. Don't you have to get sick to grow old?

The grandson of a cavalryman had special privileges in Imperial Russia. Like a freed Negro before our Civil War. So the old man grew up despising caftans and beards and Jews who prayed for help.

Max

I'm so tired, Max thought. Dirty green walls. The tank pumps in oxygen. The brown nurse looks at the dials. Skin the color of a *Zygopetalum*. A spike orchid marked with chocolate brown. Too hot here and no sun. Who can live without sun?

Who is watching my plants? The temperature must be just right. And the water. Too much and they drown. If Ben were here, he could watch for me. That Cossack boiler. It safeties and the bell rings. Rings, rings, rings. No one cares. No heat. My orchids. Flower spikes white with mauve, and white flushed with pink and spotted with crimson. And the yellows, the golden ones, the lemon-colored— no end, no end, and the *Digbyana* with its frilled lip like a Hasid's beard.

They'll all die.

Bennett

My father and I used to play fast horse, slow horse. I sat on my father's instep, facing him; his legs were crossed and he held both my hands. Slow horse—my father would rock me up and down in slow sweeping curves. *Fast horse,* I'd command, and we would change feet and his foot would pump up and down, higher and higher, until I screamed with delight and partly with fear. And he would pick me up and kiss me. Always when he saw me, he would kiss me.

Until I started school. Then the kisses stopped.

One evening, after supper, my mother said to my father, "It's time the boy went to Jewish school. He'll be twelve soon."

My father stopped drying the dishes. (An enlightened, modern man, he often said, should help in the house.) He draped the dish towel over his shoulder and held up the plate, examining it on both sides. "He doesn't need it. I'll teach him at home." Turning his back, he stacked the plate on the drainboard and picked another out of the rinse water.

"You said that when he was ten, and again when he was eleven. The girls didn't go, but I want my son to go."

My father turned to her again. "No." Then, waving the plate in his hand, "He'll be taught nonsense by fools and fakers."

"You're a stubborn man," Mama said, "but this time it's not going to be your way."

He seemed to swell up. His corded upper arms strained against the rolled-up sleeves of his gray shirt. "Listen to reason." He waved the plate for emphasis—still very quiet, he didn't believe in yelling, hated it—and the plate struck the corner of the table, broke into many pieces, and fell on the floor. The old man looked wonderingly at the piece in his hand.

My mother got up slowly, picked up a plate from the dry stack, and smashed it on the floor. Father grabbed a plate with the other hand and sent it after mother's. Mama smashed another. Gladys ran in—a book in her hand—screaming, "What's going on here?"

Father strode to the back door, opened it, and slammed it shut behind him. Mother walked over and locked the door. I drained my milk in one gulp, ran to the window, and saw him loping, like an old gray wolf, through the snow to the greenhouse.

Mama sat down with her elbows on her knees and her head in her hands, palms over her ears. She cried. Gladys threw her arms around Mama and kissed her again and again. I grabbed the dustpan, and Gladys swept the shards into the pan. Then I kissed Mama quickly on top of her head and ran back to the window, to hide my tears, pressing my head against the cold glass.

In a little while the door knob rattled. My mother dried her eyes in her apron, arose, and switched on the radio. I heard kicks, soft ones, then louder, and the door began to shiver and throb. Gladys ran to Mama. "Mama, please, please, let him in. It's snowing. He'll freeze to death!"

Finally, my mother got up and opened the door. My father walked in, snowflakes on his shirt, a puzzled look on his face. Gladys and I threw ourselves on him, kissing and hugging him. He took my mother in his arms. The four of us clung together, kissing and crying and hugging.

"I'll make some cocoa," my mother said. "It's a cold night."

It was the best cocoa I ever tasted.

The next day we went to Boston in the truck and I enrolled in a Jewish school.

In the beginning God created heaven and earth. The earth it was without form and void.

After three weeks, I had memorized these two lines; I could copy them in Hebrew in my odd-lined book, the book with a curly-headed boy in a skullcap and a black-haired girl on the cover—the back cover, since we started from the back of the book and wrote from right to left.

The bearded teacher twisted my ear one day when I was looking out the window at a tree. I told my father he had smacked me on the side of the head and made me dizzy.

"Cowards! To strike a small boy," my father said to my mother.

"Maybe he did something wrong, Max," Mama said.

"Find another school where they teach without knocking his brains out. No, never mind. I'll drive down Sunday and have a nice talk with that child-beater."

Mama wouldn't chance it and found another school. Three trolley changes this time, but only three days a week, not five. I studied there six months, starting all over again, and learned, In the beginning God created—in Yiddish this time. We were told we could believe this or not, as we wished, since this school was for free thinkers. My father was happy when he heard this until one day he asked me, to my surprise, 'What have you learned today , Ben?"

"Our class had an election, Max."

"An election? Who won?

"Norman Thomas got thirty-two votes, our president got two votes, and that other man—the sunflower man—got one vote."

"Mama, did you hear that? That's the school you found. Our President Roosevelt, an intelligent gentleman with a heart for the entire country—two votes."

"I voted for him," I said quickly.

That school was soon finished.

The next one was run by a lawyer and his sister in a storefront in the West End, a few blocks behind the statehouse. The lawyer collected four dollars a month from our parents and prepared the older boys for confirmation. His sister taught all three classes until we were turned over to him at twelve. She read stories and wrote on the blackboard and we copied. Now I went to school only on Wednesday and Sunday. Every Sunday we seemed to celebrate another holiday. We ate matzo and jam, nuts, raisins, and sometimes drank fruit punch or heavily diluted sweet wine. And if there were no holidays, there was always a basket of hard-filled candies to munch.

One day I told my mother that I would be studying with the lawyer next week to prepare for confirmation. "No bar mitzvah," my father said. "A meaningless rite inherited from unwashed goat herders."

"I've given so many presents at so many affairs," my mother pleaded. "Why can't it be our turn to receive some now?"

My father said, "No bar mitzvah!"

It was final. He never asked again what I had learned, and so I completed my Jewish education.

Max

In the morning the early sun strikes the foot of my bed and paints bars on the wall. At home I'd be up and out working. I barely remember my father, a square man, shorter than Grandpa. When I was five, my father caught his leg in a grinding wheel of the mill machinery he was fixing. Gangrene set in. They cut off his toes. He groaned in pain and no one could help him.

Toward the end, my grandfather sat in my father's bedroom. A husk of the strapping giant in our picture, he did not go outdoors any longer. He dragged out his cavalryman's blouse and sat next to Papa's bed, wearing the smelly gray rag over his pajamas. Grandpa didn't eat or sleep and hardly left the room.

One day I was noisy and my mother said stop it, stop the noise, be a good boy or your father will die.

The next day Papa died.

My mother has cried ever since I can remember. Every day she cried. At ten I was glad to go away to boarding school, an agricultural school in Toronto. My mother walked with me to the Odessa station the day I left for school. I desperately wanted her to beg me not to go; I hoped the train had broken down, the railroad ticket had been lost, anything.

Still crying, she let me go.

I had many good years, first in Canada, then Cambridge, and then raising a family in Auburndale, until, during the Depression, I lost my greenhouses. I went to work for a florist, wrapping flowers in waxed paper and selling them to rich people. Anyone who had twenty-five cents for flowers in those days was rich. Thank you ma'am, and ring up fifty cents. Then the florist ran out of customers, and I was out of work. I made wider and wider circles every day with my truck.

Finally, thirty miles north of Boston, in Beverly Farms, I found work on a big estate. The Cabots and Lodges and Pattons all lived there. The work—nothing. I can do any kind of work. But some days they needed me to chauffeur the crippled grandfather into Boston. To dress up in that monkey suit and drive him. Thank God Mama and Ben and the girls couldn't see me. I, Max Cohen, a scientific, trained agriculturist who worked in the Harvard Botanical Gardens at nineteen, who had never bent even for the Cossacks, was reduced to driving the American gentry.

I saved my money. Saw my family once a month. And four years later I was back to the work I loved. My own man.

Bennett

When I was twelve, my father pulled up to the school playground in his Reo truck. The May sun felt warm and good. I ran down the grassy slope to meet him. It would be a great day—helping my father plant shrubs at a new house in the afternoon and, later, supper in a restaurant. Then I remembered. "Max, I'm supposed to meet a boy now—he wants to fight. But I guess it can wait. We'll fight on Monday." I put one foot on the running board, but my father's open palm was raised against me.

"So boys still fight," he said. "Go ahead. I'll wait for you in the truck." He turned away and stepped into the cab, slamming the door before I could explain.

I walked around to the rear entrance. It would have been so easy to shake hands. He was smaller than me. And he was scared. His friends whooped and scuffled and urged him toward me. Someone shoved him at me. He was off balance and I hit him once. a looping right smash on the nose. He fell back, the blood spurting red down his lip. He dropped his hands to his sides. Then he raised one hand and wiped his nose with the sleeve of his white shirt. It turned red, dyed mahogany. More blood came and made an irregular line on his upper lip. I wanted to give him my handkerchief, but I turned away and went back to the truck.

Max opened the door and reached his hand out, grasping mine firmly. He pulled; my shoes just scraped the running board and I found myself beside him on the sun-warmed seat. He didn't ask me anything. We drove off.

I had a dream that night.

Charge! For Czar and Country. Charge! I gripped the white horse between my knees and galloped forward with the others. To my right a man shouted, "Kill the Turks. Kill them!" To my left a brown horse jostled mine, the rider raising his saber high, screaming "Kill the Jews. Kill, kill, kill!"

Surrounded by horses and shouting men, I was swept forward into a ravine. Dead horses and men were piled at the bottom; I stepped on them, rode over them, up the slope, scrambling over the edge. Into the forest, naked backs hanging from the trees. An icy wind caught the bodies, spun them around, turning their blue fronts toward me. I looked—Jewish bodies—cut and slashed. Red crosses on their chests and backs. Flashes of fire beyond the trees. Kill! the man on the brown horse screamed, the cry cut off; a bullet tore into his throat and he pitched out of the saddle. Ragged volleys emptied the other saddles. I was riding alone. I broke out of the trees, onto the flat brown plain. Three Turks, heads bound and curved swords whirling in glittering arcs over their heads, raced toward me.

Now I turned my horse and spurred him back to the trees. Hoof-beats drummed behind me. Almost to the edge of the sheltering woods, when coming toward me, cutting off my retreat, I recognized the Cavalryman. I reined back, waiting, then started to ride to him.

Slowly, the Cavalryman drew his saber. He pointed toward the enemy behind me. I shook my head, no. He stood up in the stirrups and raised his sword over my head. I awakened and heard the clanking of the stove grates. My father was in the kitchen.

We were the only family I knew who ate breakfast, dinner, and supper all together. My two sisters when they were home, mother, father—after washing off the black dirt from the greenhouse—and I, together in the big kitchen around the oak gate-legged table. Two leaves up for company, one leaf up for the five of us; and best of all both leaves down if the girls were away. I hated to go to high school and miss dinner with my father. And I mean dinner, not lunch; the midday meal was our big one. Father, up early, had worked five hours by noon and needed a thick soup, black bread, meat and potatoes to keep him going.

Until sixteen, I felt well-favored. Not because the girls pursued me. They didn't, and I felt clumsy and tongue-tied if I walked a girl home from school. It was my parents. I looked at my friends' parents and never found better-looking parents than my own. Most spoke better unaccented English; others were richer, had a car not a truck to go about in; a few were businessmen or storekeepers, one a schoolteacher. But next to my weatherbeaten father, they all looked sickly.

That last Passover holiday before college, I awakened late and heard my mother say, "Max, hire a roofer. Stay on the ground where you belong."

"Ben and me can do it," he replied.

"Get your own dinner, then, I can't watch. I'm taking the trolley to Boston after breakfast."

On the sloping roof, happily tearing off worn shingles with a pry bar, I could look around and see everywhere. As the wind shifted, I smelled the dried cow manure from the pile next to the tool shed. My feet inched along the two-by-four my father had hooked between the west end of the roof and the chimney. The old man climbed down the ladder for another box of shingles.

I reached the chimney and the end of the bracer and, impatient and confident, curling toes in my sneakers, I clung to the chimney with my left hand—I'm left-handed—and lifted torn shingles awkwardly with my right. Then, without thinking, I transferred the pry bar to my left hand, releasing my hold. I started to slip down over the grainy shingles. Panicking, I dropped the bar, which bounced off the roof.

I spread-eagled my body flat against the roof. The shingles scraped my cheek. I dug in with my fingers—slowed my slide. Still sliding, I felt my shirt creep out of my pants and the warm shingles scraping my belly. My body strained against the roof—kiss it—bite it—hug it. Too young to die. My feet caught on the wooden rain gutter, which moaned and sagged. I hung there, not daring to breathe.

"Don't move!" my father yelled. Out of the corner of my eye, my cheek pressed against the shingles, I could see the ladder coming along the edge of the roof. My father climbed up and helped me down. "Don't tell your mother," he said after we were sitting on the ground, his arm around me. Then he gave me holy hell for being careless, and we cleaned up the grounds the rest of the afternoon. The next day we were back on the roof.

Max

An independent boy, my Ben. He tells me, I can't work with you this year, I have my own job, delivering groceries. And he's only thirteen. Yet he loves the earth. His wildflower garden when he was ten, weeds he dug out of the woods. Silver dollars he found, and white spring beauties, wild violets and ferns. The ferns died. I warned him, but he wanted no advice from me, and nothing from the greenhouses.

And then the bandit had the nerve to ask for one of my lawn mowers to use for his customers. Old people he met delivering who wanted their lawns cut. My competitor. I gave it to him. Then he told me he was tired of repotting for me for one cent for every ten pots. But he'd do it for nothing in his spare time.

Last year, he came home from college a *mentsch*. a man. Like an ox. His shoulders finally caught up with his feet. He would help me unload the bags of fertilizer from the truck. He would run up the cleated board into the truck, lift the bag to his shoulder, run down again and into the shed. And he would go faster, my boy, and faster, until I would have to tell him, slow down, sonny. This isn't a horse race. He didn't know I saw his face when I said that. I made him happy.

Ben must come. I'll tell him everything. The little bear I raised until I had to give him away to a traveling man. More time. I thought I had more time. My oldest girl is here. Like her mother. A good plain little thing with a golden heart.

The second, Gladys, almost became a leftover. Brilliant. Ungainly. Walk proud, I told her. Stick out your chest. Don't worry about the glasses. No, she stooped to make herself smaller. I sent her for postgraduate studies to Columbia. At last, from International House in New York, she brought home a Scotch midget with a walrus moustache. We're getting married, she said. We're moving to Edinburgh when he gets his doctorate. The midget said, I'll be glad to join your religion, sir. I've studied a great deal. It's a wonderful faith. Join, join, I say. Join the human race. He tugged at the end of his moustache, very polite. I clapped him on the shoulder and called him son. Never mind, you're a member already, I told him. And he knows something, the little lord. I have two grandchildren, two handsome boys.

Max and Bennett

I looked at him. Below his tanned, wrinkled neck and sharp collarbones, a gray-white half-moon above his hospital gown. The machinery that had bought him time, green tank and motor and clear hood, lay to his right. I pulled up a chair and clasped his hand in mine; he returned the grip with surprising strength.

"I'm leaving school, Max," I blurted out.

"No, not for my sake. Put the greenhouses up for sale with Bregman, he's honest. Keep the house, tool shed, and an acre." Steadily he went on, as if he had planned this talk for a long while. "You sell the orchids, shrubs, and good stuff back to the wholesalers. Sell what you can. Now," he increased the pressure on my hand, "put up a sign. MAX COHEN—GOING OUT OF BUSINESS—FREE FLOWERS. Don't sell the perennials and annuals. You'll get next to nothing for them. Give them away." He released my hand and dropped his head back on the pillow.

"And what will you do, Max?"

"Do? I'll buy a car with red seats. Should have done it when your mother was still alive. Or I'll go to Scotland to see my grandsons. Why not?" He twisted his head to one side as if he was asking this last question of himself and trying to hear the sound of it.

I couldn't pull back now. "You don't understand, Max. I'm leaving school anyway. I don't have to follow your way, Max."

He didn't smile. "What do you want to be?"

"I don't know. Not a forester. I want to listen to myself for a while and—I'll have to find out."

He turned away from me then and curled up on his side. I got up and walked to the door, clacking my feet on the asphalt-tile floor so he would be certain to hear me. Turning around, I saw he had not stirred; his back was still toward me, his left hand thrown over his ear as if to shut out all noise.

I returned to the bedside, sat down again, and waited. The nurse stuck her head through the door. "Don't tire your father and stay too long."

"I'll be leaving soon."

My father turned back to me, piercing me with his blue eyes. "Do you have to call me Max, only Max?"

"I always called you Max."

"There are other names."

"What names? Daddy—Dad? You like those better?"

Stony-faced, he didn't answer. After a while, "When you were a small boy, you told me to call you Ben, not Bennett. I did it."

He asked for justice. No more.

The nurse called, "Visiting hours are over."

"All right, Pop." I bent over and kissed him on the cheek. "You need a shave. I'll give you one tomorrow."

Sleeping

On the eve of my fortieth birthday, I'm drinking a second cup of coffee with my wife, the kids are scattered throughout the house, and the phone rings; my wife hands it to me and a voice on the other end is describing a beautiful forest park, the voice is rising and falling from lyricism to confidential whispers, and the voice congratulates me for being so farseeing, for thinking of the future, for planning ahead. I sip my coffee standing up, leaning against the yellow kitchen wall, and I hear the prices will go up soon, the voice hardly stops for a breath, and when he says the peaceful serenity of our garden setting, the simple dignity—I say, whoa now! What are you doing to end the war in Vietnam? Silence on the other end and I slam the phone into its cradle.

I look at my wife accusingly. She calmly admits, yes, I sent the card in. We should have a plot. I won't part with you ever, she says. I'm touched. My mortal remains don't interest me, I say. We have so much to look forward to—sons-in-law and daughters-in-law and grandchildren. She looks at me, my beloved with her brown eyes. I rave, just burn me and take my ashes and scatter them on a hilltop. It's against the law, she says. There's a war going on, I say.

She repeats the story word for word, the story I told her last week. A building superintendent I employed ordered his own cremation. I gave him blood. It did not help. I put my hand over her mouth but when she kisses my palm, I let her continue. The super's wife received the ashes. She did not want to put them in the incinerator and she couldn't live with them in her apartment. She carried the ashes downstairs and put them in a desk drawer in her husband's former office. The replacement I hired brought me the earthenware urn. I was surprised he fit into this little urn because the man weighed two hundred and fifty pounds.

What did you do with the ashes? my wife says. I put them into the fertilizer spreader, I say, thoroughly mixed with five-ten-five, and returned him from whence he came. My wife believes me. Actually he's still in my safe at the office and now I must dispose of him Monday. I'll do what I said I did. I rarely lie to my wife.

A few weeks later, we plan a family picnic. I'm the youngest but the leader in these affairs. My wife empties the refrigerator and my four kids are preparing lunch assembly-line style. One butters and smears, another slips in ham or cheese or meat loaf, another cuts, another wraps. I study the map and label the sandwiches with the other hand. N.M. for no mustard. My middle brother arrives with his wife and two kids. Then my oldest brother and his second wife and my mother. They bring my mother-in-law and crippled father-in-law. It's a shirtsleeve day in June and I study the map and promise them a hemlock grove and a babbling brook to cool their feet.

We go out to the three cars and the families become hopelessly mixed. As we pull away, my car in the lead, my oldest brother following, my wife sitting next to him, my daughter announces a trifle smugly, Daddy always gets lost. I'm very careful and wait at all turns for the other two cars to pull up before I drive ahead. Somewhere south of New Brunswick, I take a turn and drive awhile and know I'm in a strange area. I take a left, hoping to pick up the main road, then I stop and back the car up and turn around and my wife is waving a message through the window of the next car but I don't heed, just go back the way I came and turn again and see a park sign, and ride along looking for another and see a large arrow and another arrow and I look back and my wife is waving again but no matter, there are lots of arrows now and up a hill onto a newly paved road, more arrows—they beckon me on, and I glance back and my brother is waving his fist at me, he always was a little stuffy but a good guy, and I go through the big iron gates and glimpse the sign Mt. Pleasant Park above the gates, but now I perversely won't turn back and the others follow and I drive on and we begin to pass the white markers and then a few large marble homes and I don't look to either side of me, just drive on and there are cars parked on the shoulders and little groups of people searching and I drive on and the paved road peters out and turns to dirt, and I see a few freshly dug holes, the red clay soil mounded on either side, and I drive on and we're in a forest park and the road comes to a halt, a dead end, and I swing the car around to face the others; it's shady here and my oldest brother's car meets mine; our headlights are face to face, and he climbs out and hugs me saying to my wife and his wife and the kids and everyone assembled around us, I told you my crazy brother Ben was taking us to the cemetery. He's laughing and I'm laughing and my mother starts to laugh and calls me a *meshigana,* and my little one asks why did Grandma call Daddy a Michigan, is that an Indian name (she had been learning about the Mandans, the Lenni-Lenapes, and the Mohawks), and my mother says no that means crazy one in Yiddish. I lower the tailgate of the station wagon and start taking out the lunch. We're still laughing and we sit and stand and eat and give everyone Jewish-Indian names and it turns out to be the best family picnic we ever had.

When the salesman called back, earnest and wary this time, he assures me he too has a social conscience and he talks about the history of the Jews and how we were slaves in the land of Egypt and when the Jews reached the Promised Land, the first thing they did was to set aside consecrated ground, holy ground for a burial plot. I silence him this time with Paramus is too far and I have a plot in Mt. Pleasant Park and I remind him of the Newark Rally Against the War and he hangs up. After all, I had purchased a picnic site and there was no reason why I should use it for anything else. I kiss my wife and hold her body against mine.

She is lying there now.

A few weeks before she left me, in the early evening, I took her hand and drew her upstairs to our bedroom. I unbuttoned the three little buttons on her collar and started to undress her. She stopped me and said the last ten years without the children home have been very good. I didn't know what to say and ran my hands over her hips. She said, I'll take off my own clothes. Do you still want the lights on? Yes, I said.

She compromised and put a lamp from the dresser on the floor and threw a yellow pillow case over it. The room was diffused in a soft amber light.

I sat on the bed, felt a twinge in my back, and bent over carefully to unlace my shoes. I slid into bed. I removed my glasses and put them on the night table. If I swim in a lake, I'm not sure I can return to shore. One cloudy day, I swam toward the clouds and turned in a panic when the sun came out and I found myself swimming away from the trees. Did she know—that I could only see the outline of her full figure as she undressed?

She got into bed and I embraced her. I rested a moment and then slipped between her accommodating thighs. She held me so tightly. The pain in my back returned. It seared me.

I'm glad now whenever that pain returns.

Even after they married, my children came occasionally with their problems. I'd listen, sometimes part with one hundred dollars, and tell them it would work itself out. Then suddenly, I became the child and my children became the father.

They advised me: get rid of that big house. I did. I divided the proceeds into five equal shares, keeping one fifth for myself. I thought I'd silence them this way. I took my wife's sewing basket, a few sticks of furniture, my file cabinets, bought a new bed, and moved back to New York.

I stay active, knowing this is important. The younger people at the meetings treat me with great respect.

Get rid of that car, Dad. It's impractical. You can rent one if you need a car. Buy a subscription ticket to Lincoln Center repertory, my children urge. Don't go into Central Park at night. I like to watch the seals. I need the car. I decide to leave it on the street to save the fifty dollars a month garage rental. Parking Monday, Wednesday, and Friday. Get up early Tuesday and move it because the street is cleaned that day. I spend three hours a day moving the car. It was stolen once. Now I have double trunk locks, double steering-wheel locks, and police siren alarms on each door. One day I forgot where I parked it. That scared me. Now I carry a little blue spiral notebook and jot down the street that the car is on. I remember everything else too clearly. Laundry machine on Tuesday; cleaner's on Friday.

Take a trip, Dad, my oldest daughter says. I remind her of the New York Monster Rally to End the War and she says you can be excused once in your lifetime. I'm reasonable and now they want to know where I'm going and where I'll stop on the way and do I have enough traveler's checks.

I drive away. I travel very short distances. Anyone following me would think I'm crazy. On the New York State Thruway and off onto rolling U.S. 20. On and off. I stop in little towns for coffee and to look at the people. Sometimes in a tavern, see a different class of people and I have a beer. Just one and drive on. The motels are all alike. Twelve units or sixteen units or twenty-four units. Pennsylvania Turnpike and Ohio Turnpike.

I stop for a swim in a state park. The sun blinds me when I walk out of the bathhouse. She used to get nut-brown in summer. She hated the cold. She'd shrink into her coat. You're the vainest man I ever met, she said. Now I'm all white, my belly a fish-colored white, and I put my clothes back on without going into the water.

I lose her in Nebraska. In California, I check in to a forty-eight-unit motel. I can't sleep and I put a quarter in the vibrator. It hums and shakes the motel bed. Supposed to soothe you and relax the muscles. We were together in Lake Placid once. Lying quietly and I slipped a coin into the machine. And she started to laugh. Couldn't do it while she was laughing. Hard luck. We weren't intimate that often anymore that I wanted to miss that one—and last night—when the humming started—I jumped out of bed—stared at it from a chair—couldn't sleep even when the bed stopped rocking.

I buy a jerry can and go through the desert. I lose her here again. Finally, I lose her and I'm glad. I think I'm glad. I stop for gas. I sweat, unbelievably. I don't see a mirage. Just drink and sweat and mop.

I'm ready for Paul Fenton and I head for Albuquerque.

Waking

I approach Fenton's studio with some apprehension. A man with impeccable credentials: he fought with the Loyalists in Spain, he knew Franz Fanon and was a major in the Algerian War of Independence, he had been purged by Senator McCarthy twice, the second time under an assumed name; we believed him when he said only a bad back kept him from joining Castro in the Sierra Maestra.

The town has grown since I was here last, mostly Spanish rococo but not Fenton's—his storefront studio sports a New York imitation black marble front with Fenton's name in gold letters. He hasn't changed much. A small wiry man with a pointed black beard, a monk's tonsure of hair around his bald head, very suntanned, and as I look down on him, I see his smooth scalp heavily covered with brown closely spaced freckles. A very strong handshake and he's asking about the old bunch. What the hell have you done, Fenton, I say, as I look around the white studio walls covered with more than fifty paintings of rabbis. Some with long white beards, other gray-speckled or black beards, and here and there an auburn beard. I recall Fenton's paintings of workers and peasants and mestizos and blacks and feel betrayed. There's a very good market for rabbis out here, he says. Why starve in New York when the Golden West wants rabbis and pays well too. Fenton smiles his little smile. Take a closer look at that one. I follow Fenton's pointing finger and stick my face very close to this rabbi's mug. It is Karl Marx with vestments. I look to the right and see Ho Chi Minh with a reddish straggly beard; to the left Castro, very recognizable to aficionados but the skullcap gives him a merry look. I turn back to Fenton and hold his small hand in both of mine, silent as I look into his eyes. He can read my admiration for his achievement. It was the only way, Ben, he says, and he joins his other hand to mine and we stand this way for a few moments, our four hands entwined.

Then the talk grows nostalgic and I remind him of our canoe trip down the Allagash and propose he join me now, close up the shop and we'll hike into the mountains together for a few weeks or months. He can't spare the time, too many commissions—really,

really sorry. He jots down the address of a good outfitter and makes me promise to stop in when I return. Then he busies himself setting up three familiar faces, one under the other on a tall easel. I embrace him goodbye and walk out. Looking back through the plate-glass window, I see him working steadily with a brush and applying whiskers to the three faces, dabbing here and there, and stepping back each time to examine the effect.

The club-footed outfitter looks skeptical when I announce that I need a complete backpacking outfit for a trip alone into the mountains. How about an exercycle? I refuse. What mountains? he asks. Idaho, I say in a flash; I had heard there were mountains there. I buy new Dunham boots, a Gerry pack frame, a Coleman stove, lots of freeze-dried foods, etc., etc. I change clothes in the store and drop my old clothes in a trash can on the way out. The rest is not very interesting: I hiked for three days—the usual rocks, flora, and fauna, oh yes, bears—there were bears. After three days I reached **The Top.** Thousands of sightseers had preceded me. The ski lift, in summer operation now, dropped off one hundred people a minute from each of the fifty states. It was crowded and dangerous at **The Top**—what with all the pushing and shoving—great danger that one might be trampled or pushed off the edge—to **The Bottom.**

Down I went, my feet hurt in the new boots, and up the next mountain. Let's get on with it now, a little faster. Down again and up another mountain and yet another. Faster! And ran out of food, and ran out of water, and was found half starving and very thirsty by a band of Indians, and told them I was searching for my totem and they didn't think it at all strange that a man almost sixty-five would be searching for his totem and they took me in and I didn't think it strange that they called themselves the *Meshiganas* even though it was in Idaho, faster now, get on with it, and they taught me rug-weaving, very restful, and I searched for my totem, they advised fasting on a mountaintop, I told them I had tried this already, and I searched for my totem, and they called me blood brother, these *Meshiganas,* and I searched for my totem and I stayed with them happily for many years. Oh, I forgot to mention that when I lived with the Indians, I baked unleavened bread on the rocks and subsisted on a healthful diet of fruit and nuts. I gave up smoking. No, I did not take a squaw into my wigwam to live with me as that other fellow did in the movies, faster now, tell it all, I searched for my totem. I lived alone.

They gave me the usual peace pipe when I left. I promised to write often. They gave me the usual deerskin clothes, chewed to a rare suppleness, and the usual beaded moccasins.

The car at the foot of the mountain wouldn't start.

I begin walking away from the mountain, away from the car. The sun rises and I walk toward it, knowing that is a direction. My throat is parched and the pack is heavy. I sweat and drink from my canteen. I unfasten the clips and cast the pack off without looking back. The empty canteen flaps against my hip. Good fellows, the *Meshiganas,* but much time wasted with them. I consult my own. I once read **The Book** and now I call on Solomon, David, and Saul. Or was it Saul, David, and Solomon? Good kings every one, but absent-minded; they do not know which one arrived first. There are other books: Testaments, Talmuds, Scrolls, and Manifestos, but it's too late now. I tramp along and my wife appears and skips alongside. She tells me her visions: Standing in front of one hundred students, she says, I couldn't remember a math proof. One I've done again and again. I saw the diagram. But couldn't do it.

Now she skips around to my left; she's wearing her jonquil-colored wool bathing suit and I see the little hole in the suit, on the curve of her right hip; I stretch one hand out to tickle the white flesh but she stays out of reach. The clear daylight flows between her thighs. She starts another tale: Our furniture was all in the street. Green sofa, kids, beds, everything—and various dump trucks, cranes, other equipment was marching across our front lawn. I dressed hurriedly, she says, and ran down to the construction shack set up next door. The man there, a dark Mafia type, said, I told your husband to buy road-building insurance—he wouldn't listen.

I walk faster, my feet sink into the sand. I'm crossing the Red Sea and still she skips along, growing older, legs still great though, and she tells another vision, surprising me: I who thought always I had all the dreams. Husband mine—you and I and the two children: I was pregnant (triplets), we were driving to the New Jersey shore along the Garden State Parkway. In our second car, dearest, you remember—the huge Chevy station wagon (Bluie, I remembered, we called that car Bluie) you bought so we'd have room for all our kids. We were stopped by many armed soldiers, men and women carrying rifles. Our kids yelled, make Bluie fly, Dad, make her fly. To the right, in front of twelve toll booths, there stood a big white house with green shutters and a long open porch on the second floor. A line of soldiers on the platform, rifles pointing toward us. Shots rang out. People scrambled out of their cars and threw themselves on the ground, behind their cars, anywhere. Ben, you were standing tall on the roof of our Chevy and shaking your fist. I pulled you down beside me. The asphalt was very hot. I hung on to your neck; the children sheltered between us. The new babies—all three—kicked—inside me. I looked up at the sky. It was very blue. I decided that was the last thing I wanted to see—

People screamed—

I guess **The War** is still going on. Once, I needed the scissors. To trim some old leaflets, a little yellow and brittle but still serviceable. **End The War,** the leaflets said. Where's the scissors? I yelled. I had told my wife a thousand times not to touch the scissors. Begged her to leave them in the night table next to our bed. My wife's not there. If she were, she'd never answer if I shouted. I tried her sewing basket. I opened it and under a pile of socks (just single ones; my wife, **God Bless Her,** never sewed socks; she just threw the holey ones out, and saved the good ones). She said, since I only used black or brown, she'd make up pairs from the good ones and put them back in my sock drawer. The clever, sexy little devil, I loved her so, she never bothered with non-essentials, what a load of socks.

Did she understand the day I ran upstairs, out of breath; I couldn't wait to tell her: I had seen an old man that morning giving out leaflets and he had haunted me all day, I could hardly work, and again at night he was still there at the subway station or he had gone away and returned to catch the evening crowd and the old man was papyrus-thin and gaunt and he is me, he is me—there is no mistake about it and she looked at me that day, in such a way that I would never leave her, I would never leave her.

I see Semiramis. She looks so frail, Semiramis, my beloved wife, as she holds up a net sack of onions in one blue-veined hand and she says in her cigarette-wracked sexy voice: Imagine, Ben! The price of onions. Just imagine! Two pounds of onions for eighty-five cents. How do people live today?

Joshua in the Rice Paddy

We'll all move to Canada, my oldest sister said.

The *Chronicle* had reported Gordon, my father's prize shot-putter on the high school track and field team, missing in action. Mother said to me, I hope the war will be over before you—and she got up to stir the stew. My little sister threw her arms around my neck. I'll hide you in the woods and bring food every day. I want to serve my country, I said, my fourteen-year-old bass breaking into treble on the last word, and then looked at my father's Mohawk face for some clue. He stared out the window at the bird feeder.

He named me Joshua, after my grandfather in Glasgow. I never met him, even though my grandfather had dishonored us by changing his name from Weinfeld to Winfield. So change it back, I told him. It's too late, he said.

There's a picture of Mom and Dad on their bureau that I like to study. Dad's in his British wooly air force uniform, the jacket a size too small, and his arm is around my mother; she's smiling and has that perky turned-up Waves hat on, looks about nineteen, admits she was twenty-four; they met at a dance in London, married as soon as he was mustered out, and he followed her to New Jersey. He worships her. My mother says openly she joined the Waves to find a man. She got Bernie and adores him. They still laugh that my sister was a six-month baby and weighed nine pounds. Mom went to work as soon as she could and Dad worked as a mason and then finished college. He teaches health and physical education in the next town and says it's better than being a gravedigger like his father or a part-time rabbi like his grandfather, a specialist in funeral orations.

Listen to my father. He won the war singlehanded, shooting down Germans from his rear gunner's seat, right and left. Under pressure, he'll admit he got a little help from Americans like Colin Kelly and Levin, the Jewish bombardier. But no one else. The War? What war? We've had so many. The Korean War. Dad hardly knows it happened. The Vietnam War—he's just beginning to see it, after all these years. Dad talks about The War, The War, and he expects you to know which one he means.

I was just a little guy, eight or so, when he took me to the Highland Games in Metuchen. I'll never forget that day: Dad in his red plaid vest and green tam-o'-shanter; the marching bagpipe bands, the red-kneed girls and brawny men in their kilts; the puffed-out straining cheeks and the wild cries of the pipes. Then a jumping contest with the lean men trying to reach a sheaf of wheat without knocking over the crossbar; the crumbly oat cakes and steaming chocolate, and cotton candy and custard. I could have anything I asked for that day. And best of all: tossing the caber. Strong young men in shorts, hard-bellied older men, a few my dad's age; they'd pick up this telephone pole in both hands, balancing it on their shoulders, start slowly and then speed up until they were trotting, the wavering pole resting on one shoulder, up to the starting line and one gut-wrenching heave and the pole would turn over, flip through the air and hit the ground with a thud. Sometimes a pole tipped backwards, torn by its own weight from the thrower's hands as he ran to the line, and there was loud friendly laughter from the stands. A gray-haired man took third place. I couldn't bother my father—these were sacred moments. When the winner was called to the judges' stand, he had enough and we went home.

That night his friends, red-faced Buckles and hump-backed Gallagher, came over and they all sang: My heart belongs to Glesgee/To dear old Glesgee toon/ When I have a bottle with a drap in't/Glesgee belongs to me. Roaring drunk they were. I listened from the top of the stairs and my mother went down to grab the bottle and came upstairs with it, but maybe they had another because they kept shouting and singing until I fell asleep to the lilting promise of "Road to the Isles."

The following week my father went into serious training in the basement with weights and pulleys and he made my mom sew a Star of David on his sweatshirt. And one day my father said, come on, you'll help me find a caber and I'll practice and win the games next year or place anyway. I followed him and we searched for a fallen tree of the proper size. Here's one, Dad, I said. Sure enough, he started lopping off the side branches, made the chips fly; he could handle an ax, all right. Then he picked up the tree and hefted it. We carried it, one of us at either end, to a clearing and he practiced a few throws. He finally got the hang of running with it, managed to loft it a few times but never could get it to go end over end, the only way you can get distance with a caber. After a while, he just forgot about the caber and began instructing me in soccer. He really could head that ball; he coached the high school team and I'd ride with him in the big yellow bus to all of the out-of-town games.

MANY YEARS AGO. I punched Police Lieutenant Kajadian's kid in the stomach. He pushed me at recess and I turned around and gave him one shot in the belly. How was I to know he had a weak stomach? He caved in and they carried him to the nurse.

The principal called Mother to school. My father said he'd handle it. He asked for the facts. I told him. He took a half-day off and came home at lunchtime. After a second bath, he dressed carefully in his Scottish tweed jacket, red plaid vest, and green tam-o'-shanter. He used lots of shaving lotion so he'd smell good. He told me to wait for him and we'd go back to school together. I told him, you just tell 'em how it happened, Dad. He gave the V sign and I walked proudly next to him, striding to stay abreast, to the martial squeal of the pipes, to the principal's office where Dad motioned me to sit down on the bench outside. He squared his shoulders, straightened his tie, and marched in.

It's the first fight I ever had and Joe was my good friend. I didn't know he had a weak stomach. The door was open a crack and I strained to hear. Sometimes I heard my father's voice: just scraps. I raised him peacefully. The principal's low calm voice: a school building—can't permit violence. Respects other people, my father said. My teacher louder: he must be taught—hooliganism—some punishment at least. My father's voice over hers: this is a violent world. I don't want him to be aggressive but he has the right, yes, the duty to defend himself. Someone shut the door and I could hear no more.

My father came out and took my hand. He slapped his tam on at a rakish angle. Is it all right? I asked. Yes, he said. Don't hit anyone first but if they hit you, strike back—fast, fifty or sixty times— and then talk it over later. I never had another fight, and hope I never will.

JOSHUA FIT THE BATTLE OF JERICHO. I won my first wrestling match in the intramural tournament. I won a second. I won a fourth against a stocky guy who's working out with the Junior Varsity. You don't have to be a wrestler, son, Dad said. It's a good clean sport. Builds all the muscles evenly. But you don't have to. Basketball is O.K. too, he said, making a wry face.

That night, after my fourth victory, I slipped behind the old man and grabbed him in a nelson. He's out in a second and I'm on the floor, my nose pressed into the dusty rug, his legs are around my waist and he's squeezing the breath out of me. He'll kill me if he can. I know he will. He let up and pulled me to my feet. I'm sorry, he said, over and over. He looked pale and sick. I told him it's my fault, I started it. He'd kill me, I know it. I'm sorry, he said. I'm thirty pounds heavier. Forget it, Dad. He'll kill me.

To take his mind off it, I showed him a poem I had written. It ended: A hand swept over the blackboard/ and the story yet to be written—erased. My teacher asked how the story could be erased even before it was written. My father said to me, you're a poet. He took out his worn copy of Bobby Burns and read a long poem aloud, "A Man's a Man for A' That." I couldn't follow it too well because of the Scotch burr my father deepens when he reads Burns. While he read I thought about a story I had read or heard—I couldn't remember which. It tells of a boy who used to wrestle with his father. As the boy grew taller and stronger, his father became paunchier and weaker. In their final wrestling match, the father was in control at first but his young son gradually overcame him, pinning him to the ground, shouting DO YOU GIVE UP! DO YOU GIVE UP!!! Later, outside the house, the father broke down and cried.

A FIRESIDE CHAT. What are you doing, Dad? No answer. He just changes his swing. The two black chairs he was swinging out and down to his side are now swinging toward me and down. He's breathing hard. Why in the hell are doing that?

If I meet a middle-aged Nazi, changing his swing again, out and down go the chairs, and he's not in condition—he holds both chairs at arm's length, steady, his shoulders corded—I'll kill him.

Keep it up. You'll get a heart attack.

Don't hassle me. Do I hassle you? He always starts using my slang just as it's getting dated. If you were observant, the old man says, putting both chairs down and leaning on the curved ladder backs, you'd see I'm using kitchen chairs now and they're a couple of pounds lighter than the dining-room chairs. He sits down, switches on the record player, and raises his paper in front of his face. It's "Dream Angus"—I know them all—and live your own life, I hear.

JOSHUA GETS HIS LETTER. He gave it to me. Aren't you going to open it, he says.

I know what it is, I say.

You're on your own. I'm not wrapping you in cotton wool and taking you down to a draft counselor like some parents. You know how to find one, if you want one. Good one in Plainfield, I heard at the Friends' meeting. I can't tell you what to do. It's your ass. Are you going to open it now, he says later in a very quiet voice.

I know what's in it, I say.

JOSHUA GROWS HIS HAIR. I let my hair grow long. My father offered me money for a haircut. First time he'd done this since I started earning my own spending money. He wears his hair like a marine drill sergeant. My father coaxes, cut it just a bit, just to clean up, maybe trim it a bit.

I tell him Samson wore his hair long and look what happened to him when he cut it. My mother says I look more and more like my father every day. We turn back to back and my mother says, Dad is only an inch taller now.

Unexpectedly my father says, I'm glad you're letting your hair grow long. I don't want you to copy me. Can I believe him?

FIRST MAN ON THE MOON. Come in and watch it, Dad, I say. A blinding spear of light. You can see it twenty miles from Cape Canaveral.

Horsedung, he says. It's done with mirrors and ultraspectroscopy, infrared rays and inverted telescopic high-beam cameras. The Nix does it with mirrors. All staged in a bomb-proof vault under the Pentagon.

They'll land on the moon, I say.

It's a bloody fake, he says. A bloody fake. Like the king and queen and all the bloody princes and princesses, all fornicating and breeding more bloody fakes.

I say, maybe you're right, Dad. After they get out of sight, they'll turn it around and head for Nam and bomb the piss out of the little skinny brown men. I shut the television set off. The image of the rocket stays on the dark screen for a few seconds. My father looks like he is getting ready to puke.

JOSHUA AND BERNARD. He's not sleeping lately. I hear him up at five A.M. every morning. Where are you going, Bernie? I call out through my closed door.

Did you call me Bernie? he says.

I called you Bernie.

It's the first time, he says.

There's a first time for everything.

Cliché, he says.

Where are you going and who are you today?

I'm taking my claymore, laddie, and going into the heather.

What are you looking for, Dad?

I don't know, laddie, I don't know.

The next day, I look at my watch—5:00 A.M. and he's stirring again. I'm all right, I hear him say to my mother, just you go back to bed. Where are you going, Dad? I call out.

Out, he says.

Why? Where?

I'm going to buy a high-powered rifle, he says. I used to be a crack shot. First I'll kill the king and queen, then Nix, then HO-HO-HO, then LAM PHAM DUC and then DUC PHAM LAM, then Stalin, but he's dead already, and Chancre Jack, he's lived too bloody long.

The old man's politically naive. I jump out of bed and rush into the hall. He searches my face. I'll be okay, he says. You want to do something useful? Put up some coffee; I'll be back soon.

I shout after him, take the dog too while you're going, slipping on my pants and buttoning up as I follow him down the stairs. Dad, I call out again, and he turns back with one hand on the door knob. Son, I'm going down to the draft board and chain myself to the radiators and eat the key.

For Chrissakes Dad, cut it out. . . .

If I'm not back by noontime, ask mother for the duplicate. Come down and release me, 'cause I want to be back in time for lunch.

Dad! Dad! I hear the door slam. The dog runs to the door, howls and rises up on her hind legs and rakes the door with her front paws.

JOSHUA VISITS A SICK FRIEND. The dayroom was a high-ceilinged, bare, tan tile room with a dark-brown tile border. They locked the door after they let me in. Six boys were watching TV in one corner of the room, four of them in brown bathrobes. Two guys in jeans were shooting billiards on a soft warm green table. A black attendant in a soiled white uniform walked through a blank door at the far end of the room and pulled up one of the green tubular plastic-covered chairs and sat down to watch television.

I walk over to Herby, who is by himself in one corner, wearing a fancy blue bathrobe over his bluejeans, his bare feet in moccasins. Herby gets up, a big smile on his face when he sees me; a book on his lap falls to the floor. I shake his hand and get right down to it. Come on, Herby. Get dressed and get out of here.

How's your father? he says, and points to a chair. I sit too suddenly and bounce up and down on the spring tube chair.

How's Bernie the Bombardier, he says.

Come off it, Herby. Let's stick to your problems.

They kill you out there, Herby says matter-of-factly. I'm not coming out. Writing any poetry?

Some. . . .

Herby picks up the black-covered paperback at his feet. He holds it up and I read: Where is Vietnam?—American Poets Respond. He opens the book and begins to read: My name is Joshua. My letter appeared in the *Wayne University Collegian*, Detroit, Michigan: The world is not Americo-centric/ and we are participants in a world community/ not masters of it. Did you write that, he asks me?

I shake my head from side to side. I'm sure he's not reading, just made it up.

He goes on: In South Jersey/ Across the land of the Lenni-Lenapes/ Lived Bouncing Bernie: El Bombardero/ With his Laddie, Samson Weinfeld/

Come on, Herby, I interrupt him, get dressed.

No, Joshie Boy. Come around when it's over. He closes the book and stares at his lap.

What time do you get up in the morning, Herby?

Anytime at all. Ten-Twelve-Two. Anytime.

After that we have nothing else to say and I leave him.

JOSHUA ALONE. I'm dreaming about my friend Richard. Clear as can be, I see his name in big block letters in the *Chronicle* obituary column. I awaken and sit up, take several deep breaths. Not Richard. Not him. He grew a beard and it came in scraggly, made him look homelier than ever. After three years on the high school track team, three years of daily practice, he got into a meet and came in eighteenth. Never higher than eighteenth. Somebody must remember Richard.

I'm tossing around and trying to get back to sleep when I hear Dad's bagpipe records blasting downstairs. Then Hatikvah, the Jewish national anthem, and when it ends I recognize "MacPherson's Lament." Then silence and I don't like the quiet either so when I hear the door slam I get up and come down.

He's slouched in his favorite walnut chair, legs spread out, next to his beloved record player. I'll put out the garbage, I say, and scoot into the kitchen, grab the overflowing bag, and go down the side steps. I lift the can cover and see a broken record lying on top. I pick it up—why it's my father's favorite, "Road to the Isles"—and I hold it in my hand and I can hear the skirl of the pipes, the stirring martial music, the roll of the drums, and under this record five or six more: "Blue Bonnets over the Border," "Macpherson's Lament," all smashed as if a heel has pressed the garbage down and cracked the lot.

I come back in and seat myself on the rug in front of him.

That's a good lad, he says, you put out the garbage.

I give him his words back. It's good for a lad's character. Any lad who puts out the garbage for ten years can become president.

I faked you out, son, he says harshly. I never shot down any planes. Worked on the ground crew. I only went up a few times. Never saw an enemy place when I was in the air. I never should have told those lies. That air force captain I beat in a wrestling match. He didn't weigh 225 pounds. More like 180.

But you were under fire, I say.

And he wasn't a wrestler, just a football player. What did he know? I was in air raids and that's all. I soiled my underwear the first time. He rubs his eyes. And those other stories, mostly lies. Play-acting, just as bad.

Did you ever toss the caber, Dad?

Just those few times in the woods with you. You were eight years old. And I never made the British Empire Track and Field Team in the javelin, like I told you. Never got past the preliminaries.

That's O.K. too, Dad.

He wipes his eyes with the back of his hand.

Can I get you a drink? I say. A shot of brandy, Scotch? You were a good father, Dad. He doesn't hear me. You are a good father. He cups his hands over both eyes and I hurry into the kitchen, bend down and take the brandy out of the cabinet, next to Mom's cook-books. I pour a small one for me and a double for Dad and wait a few minutes looking out (he's forgotten to hang the bird feeder; it's bleak out there, not a bird in the air or on the bare sassafras tree), and wait a bit more before I'll go back into the living room.

I give him the brandy. I didn't believe every word, I say. He brightens a little, turns the glass around, looks into it. I liked them anyway. They were good stories. How about my draft call, Dad—I can claim C.O. status. What do you think?

I don't know, he says.

Or I can duck out and take off for Canada.

I don't know.

Or take my chances. It's got to be over soon. Everyone doesn't get killed. Do you mind if I ask you all these questions, Dad?

I don't mind, son. How are you going to learn if you don't ask your father questions? His oldest joke.

I get up from the rice paddy. The sergeant is yelling for us to head for higher ground, the helicopters are coming in. Doubled up, I move forward. The last thing my father said that night was you can't toss the caber in a rice paddy. A burst of fire off to one side; I'm knocked off my feet and lying there in the warm water, I hear the sweet sound of the pipes again and the muffled roll of the drums, and I see the dirty water stained a deeper swirling brown.

King Henry

It's hard to shun a man who seems to admire you. I can't stay away
from the wrestling room although I've given up the showering and
all that, twenty years ago. He's always there, bouncing on the black
mat on his short legs—I've never seen him lose. No more than five
feet tall, barely reaches my shoulder, shaven head, and he turns his
face to one side, the good side, when he speaks or stands in the
shadows, watching.

I see him approaching and duck into the steam room. Into the
hot, close fog, I drop onto the lowest bench, head between my knees,
hands cupped over my face, trying to breathe. The door opens and
then slams shut on its heavy spring. A man scampers up the benches
to the top, slides over to my side, and sits down. "Hank," his voice
floats down, "vunderful man, your fellow Kissinger. He's getting
things done."

I hesitate; heard his name, Rudy, at the front desk. But he's never
called me by name nor have I ever replied to him when he's tried to
speak to me before. "I don't trust anyone who speaks without
moving his lower lip."

"Vat?"

"Mr. Rotten appointed him so he's not my man."

(To myself). *Grossmutter,* the yellow Star of David, *Closely
Watched Trains,* heavy German furniture shipped to the upper West
Side one step ahead of the Nazis—all of these things don't make him

my man. "He can kiss my ass. Henry Kissinger can KISS MY ASS! In fact, I always think of him as Henry KISSMYASS."

Without breathing any more deadly vapor, I jump up, stiff-arm the heavy door, and hurry to the locker room. I hastily towel myself dry, dress, and head for home.

I like men who bathe. They soak in warm water, take their ease, contemplative men, can even sip a cup of coffee on the edge of the tub. Soap all over. Dunk. Soap again. Dunk, then lie back head against the curved tub top and relax. Not like the showerers. These yeomen beat their hairy chests in the shower, hollering, "God for Henry, England, and Saint George!"

I missed my bath tonight. Carry the locker-room odor with me. My wife and I rushed through dinner to make an eight o'clock curtain.

An English knight storms out of the wings, shouting, "On, on to the breach." He trips over my feet (we're first row, side seats); then leaps over my legs onto the stage. Others follow coiffed in iron hats with earlaps and carrying sheet-metal-over-plywood shields. Swords raised high, whooping, they run across the stage and climb the French battlements on a hastily erected siege ladder.

Everyone's impressed by Shakespeare's heroic king. Kindly, principled, yet ruthless when he dispatched the three traitor earls and magnanimous when he gave a gloveful of sovereigns to the commoner whom Henry met while disguised.

"What a presence," my wife breathes, blowing into my right ear.

"He's Henry the *Meshigana*," I reply. "The Nut. He has England and wants France too. Imitate the action of the tiger (you heard him, dear); stiffen the sinews, summon up the blood, and impose his will on Vietnam!"

At intermission, in the chlorophyll-scented men's room, shuffling in line toward a urinal, I note three fellows, seriatim, zip their flies with their right hand and hit the flush handle at the same time with their left. I marvel at the economy of the gesture; like reaching for a man's right wrist with your left and then swiftly hooking your right under his right armpit, an ankle kick, and if it's done right—zip, flush—down he goes.

King Henry marries his French queen, Kate, and I'm driving home, sturdy Jewish wife at my side, when it starts to rain. Twist the windshield wiper dial, turn on heater and defroster, and encapsulated in the warm, safe comfort of the front seat, I remember how I tried to escape.

My boss, Paul Safro, C.P.A. who hired me to add columns of figures—figures that others had already tallied—said, "Greenberg, change your name and you'll double your income." He paid me fifty cents an hour when the Franklin Delano Roosevelt minimum wage was thirty-five cents. I'm sure he didn't intend to pay one dollar. When I asked for a ten-cents-an-hour raise, he mourned my predecessor, his lost junior, Alvin. "That boy," he said, "will become a captain in the Finance Corps in no time." Yet I heeded his advice and became Henry Green. I liked the color green: green trees, green grass, green sea.

Armed with Green, I married tall, buxom Agnes, a lay worker for the Salvation Army whom I picked up at the Red Brick; then she joined Ethical Culture and when last heard from she was sewing vestments for a cashiered priest who had joined the Catholic Workers' movement and really had no need for vestments unless he intended making a comeback. It's all vanity!

Call it a misstep, that's all. Yet I moved in the right direction afterwards. I married Daisy Klein, an Anglo-Jewish bird. The way it oughta be. Now another fellow changed names from Heinz to Henry, sloughed off a nice Jewish wife and two kids, and became Secretary of State. "My life in Furth," he once told a German reporter, "seems to have passed without leaving any lasting impressions. I can't remember any interesting or amusing moments." Didn't the young Nazis of Furth (where, after the war, only 70 of 3,000 Jews turned up alive), didn't they chase young Heinz down the streets yelling "Fatso, Fatso, Juden, Juden, Raus, Raus!"?

If a *New York Times* reporter should interview me about my life in Brooklyn, I'd tell him how it was. I used to dream that the Nazi tanks were rumbling down West Ninth Street while my friends and I cowered behind furniture-barricaded windows, machine guns ready. My friend Norman ran from a doorway to retrieve his white spitz, who barked at the iron treads of a tank. He scooped up the dog, slipped, and the tank revved its motor and rolled over him; then backed up, leaving a red-etched pancake in the gutter. I don't dare repeat this to my wife again: she's already said, it was worse in the blitz in the Midlands, and you're hopelessly neurotic, and you Americans had it easy.

Turning into our driveway, I park and see my Airedale's square jaw silhouetted in the narrow glass strip of the entrance door. I test this on Daisy. "Just mark these watersheds in my life. One, I quit wrestling. Two, ever since Kintish, that bull of a man, caught a heart attack jogging around the Central Park Reservoir, I've lost my enthusiasm. Yet it's good for me, I think."

"Stop mourning," Daisy says. "You'll do for all ordinary purposes."

When my wife's cocker spaniel died, I persuaded her to buy a brindle Airedale for protection. Airedales have guts. I saw one tackle a Great Dane twice his size. I'm a Russian wolfhound, six feet one inch, but I've always wrestled shorter fellows about five-eight to five-ten.

I kick my green-and-white jogging shoes aside and change to a comfortable half-boot; then leash my Airedale, Sasha, and with the leather phylacteries wound three times around my palm, I head for the river. I jog fifty feet with Sasha straining at the leash, walk a few hundred, and trot fifty again. Turn right on Bluff Street, along the river, and I see advancing on me a man driving very slowly (I've never spoken to him, only know him from the cigar tip that glows in his mouth); he drives with his right hand and from his left dangles a long leash out the window. At the end of this leash, a German shepherd trots arrogantly next to the car. I hold Sasha on a tight rein. The car swerves toward me. I step back and off the road onto the grassy river bank; below, the river runs dark and deep. The shepherd strains on his leash, lips drawn back, snarling, and Sasha surges to meet him. A jousting of long snout versus square jaw, savage growls from the shepherd as both dogs rise on hind legs— Sasha draws back, then charges low and hits his foe, shoulder to chest. The car picks up speed, pulling the shepherd until he is racing alongside. Twice I've wrestled German shepherds. I hate them: shaven-headed, mean-spirited, and unsporting.

Back in the house, I unleash the dog and take the steps two at a time up to my Daisy. She's brushing her teeth in front of the bathroom mirror, ready for bed. I pat her flank, run my hand over the curve of her belly, press against her, kiss the tip of her ear.

"Silly old sod," she says, "I'm whacked."

I follow her into the bedroom, begin to undress as she gets into bed, and drop my clothes in a heap on the floor. Stand in my shorts, belly sucked in, hopeful. "I believe it's the sexual urge that's behind everything. Bombs, Nam, taking care of lepers, power, lynchings, Watergate, massive sculptures, gangland slayings, everything—"

"You can't cozen me that way—"

"No, no, of course not. The theory is derivative out of Erikson, the secret Jew, but I go further, can explain everything. I can explain Hitler, Ghandi, Einstein, Nixon—all of them, just by concentrating on THE SEX!" I drop my drawers. Look down and switch out the light. I place one knee on the bed, my wife's back is turned; I've done the right thing, married Jewish. I sniff my Jewish wife. "I don't really have to have it."

"I don't work negatively, either—"

"He asked for foul sexual practices, I'm sure."

"Who?"

"Kissinger. K's wife said, nice Jewish wife that she is, Henry, I'll give you all the clean normal sex you want but none of that perverted stuff." I jounce the bed with my knee. "Henry said, get the whips, the feather boas, put on those leather boots. His wife said, no, Henry dear. He said, Hitler was— She said, you were going to say Hitler was right about you people, weren't you Henry. Admit it. I can read your mind." I look at the curve of my wife's hips. "Henry said, ve are finished! Vat you vant, I don't vant; vat I vant, you don't vant."

"How long will you continue storytelling," my wife mumbles. "So he married that chinless Gentile. Is he happy now?"

I back off the bed and step on my underwear. Catch the underwear with my right toe, kick, and flick it up, and it sails over my wife's back to rest on the floor, on her side of the bed.

I go to the window and adjust the venetian blinds. I know the sugar maple's leaves are turning yellow but the streetlight casts them in pale green shadow. I smell smoke. Even here they're burning. Flames shoot up from an open-wire trash can in the county park across the street.

Daisy lies in bed under the white sheet. I tell her, "Henry gets his orders through Nancy's diaphragm which is bugged by her old boss, Rockefeller."

Finally she says, "Concentrate on us."

I lift the sheet and slip into bed. Slide my hand under my wife's shoulders. Conjure up Nancy K, unbutton the tiny pearl buttons of her bodice but that's all as I'm thwarted by her knickers. I smell smoke. The Airedale clatters up the stairs and whines at the closed bedroom door. I wonder if Henry dares take off all his clothes. My wife's hands knead my shoulders. Our feet become entangled in the sheet and I kick it off. Hands roughen my back. I close my eyes. Hands draw the sheet back over the two of us. I thrash about. Recall the mortuary I walked into, in the cemetery, looking for a men's room. The bathroom door was locked. Spied a long slate bathtub on iron legs and a corrugated chute leading into the tub. A stack of pine coffins, ceiling-high, in one corner. Desperate, I pissed behind the coffins. Have the wrong urge now. Sasha settles down with a sigh outside the bedroom. That Rudy at the gym—vat does he vant—was he the assistant who selected the right mallet or pincers for the job? He said to me once, his back turned and crouching to tie his shoe-laces, you're in vunderful shape for a man your age. I didn't answer. I blot him out. My wife cries, happy yelps; sighs deeply, groans ugh, ugh, ugh—the phone rings, rings. Will not stop and I become enamored and thrust with each ring—thirteen, fourteen, fifteen. My wife gasps, wrong number. I murmur, should have left phone in the hall.

I throw off the covers and hop out of bed. She rests back naked and unconcerned. Unaware of her narrow escape. I gaze at her peaceful flesh, the un-English plumpness of her middle-eastern hips. The venetian blind stripes her body with green light. Then I see her walking barefoot with other naked women, hands raised high, mouths open, shame on their faces—a fuzzy, grainy newsphoto—I turn away.

"I am fulfilled," she says, "so go to the bathroom and let's get some sleep."

On Sunday, I check my weight on the balance scale after a sensible swim. I wander out; two towel-wrapped athletes nod curtly at me as I find myself drawn to the wrestling room. I peer in. The barbells and black weights are scattered on gray canvas mats to the right. Ahead, the overhead spots shine brightly on the black wrestling mat. A thick-bodied man-boy is doing pushups on the wooden floor. He gets up, rotates his shoulders, shakes his hands limply from the wrists.

To the left one light is out, and here, in the dimmest part of the room, a man in black tights sits, back resting against the wall mats. The man uncoils, and in one fluid movement is on his feet. It's Rudy, and I draw back from the doorway.

He drops his towel and walks to meet his opponent at the inner white circle. They shake hands and close, hand to elbow and hand to neck. Down they go, on hands and knees and up again. Rudy lunges for an inside leghold; his foe pulls back, brings his weight forward, shoots both hands under Rudy's armpits and counters. I remember hearing Rudy say he knew six different ways to kill a man with his bare hands: the side of the hand to the jugular, the kick to the vitals, thumbs to the throat, knee in the small of the spine . . . just preliminaries these, he knew lots more. No sound in the room but the scuffling of feet on the rubber surface.

I see Rudy's corded back; the helmet top of his opponent nestles on Rudy's shoulder; they circle with a slap-slap of feet and the other's back is facing me, a smooth, strong, beefy back, and I gaze through him, past them both—

I was wrestling a whipcord-strong man a shade taller than me. With one sweep he caught me in a headlock and bar-arm, twisted me to the mat, and I was pinned. Other silent wrestlers sat along the walls. I was humiliated, never had been pinned so quickly before. Also, I'd sworn if I ever got out of this army alive, never to shower again. BATHS ONLY in my future. This happened once—in a midwestern city—forget the name—in the army—a layover, between trains, needed exercise—hunted out a turnverein—fifteen pairs of struggling figures on the mats—all stopped to watch us. A coin tossed. I chose top position. He dropped to all fours. I crouched behind, on my knees. I embraced a steel cable. A starting slap on the mat. He stood up. From behind, I jammed my left hand into his crotch, grasped my right wrist, and rushed him off the mat. Again he rose, tried to tear my fingers away from around his waist, and I hustled him off, this time bounced him into the canvas wall protectors. I heard the chant, stalling, stalling, from the seated wrestlers. There was a gap between the wall mats—concrete gray wall. We started on the ground again; he stood, switched; I blocked and ran him off the mat. At the last moment, something turned him away from the wall mat into the concrete wall. Smashed! When I stepped back and released my grip, he crumpled to the wooden floor. I dropped to my knees and looked at his sealed eyes.

Rudy is spread-eagled across his opponent, applying a crotch and half-nelson. Pins him.

Sunday afternoon is for the *New York Times.* We sit on the couch, paper between Daisy and me, sipping coffee. More and more often now, I find myself agreeing with their sonorous editorials. So I abandon the *Times* to examine Kissinger's environment. In his office, there is a huge canvas in tones of purple undulating out of a central mushroom cloud. Also, a large still life of a bouquet of multicolored flowers presented by Leonid Brezhnev; the Chinese gave him a scroll copy of a horse painted by Hsu Pei-hung. On the table behind his desk is a framed photograph of the President; "To Henry Kissinger," says the inscription, "for whose wise counsel and dedicated services far beyond the call of duty I shall always remain grateful." From his friend, Richard Nixon. On the desk, a direct telephone to the President. I look for clues.

That night he's everywhere: on a low-flying flight from Newark airport, in the steam pipes humming vat, vat, vat, sizzling through the electric wires, can't escape him. My wife turns toward me, her hands clawing at my shoulders, "Oh, Henry."

"What did you call me?"

"You shook me out of a sound sleep. Henry, that's your name, isn't it?"

"I told you when we first met, never to call me Henry." I shove her with my hip. "Call me Hank! And you're pushing me off the bed." Silently, she opposes her hip to mine, shoves back. "Can't I have a small corner for myself?"

"Do you want twin beds?"

Now I don't answer but know finally, am almost certain: the perfect disguise. Hedging against a mishap, in their search for the final solution, they decide that Göring's illegitimate child will be planted in Furth. False identity papers, passport, history, and they invent K's parents, his grandparents, find twelve Jews to pose as his relatives (promise them passports to America), and kill the twelve in the camps. All fiction. And so he is born, comes here in 1938, and now is ready to rule/destroy the world.

I can't sleep so I get up stealthily and run a warm bath and relax in the tub. I let myself go and piss in the rising waters. And yet I wonder, recalling a friend in military intelligence during World War II who shared a pup tent with Kissinger.

"What did he say?" I asked.

"*Grobe Gott,* iss it cold in here, in this *verdammte* tent!"

"That's all? Nothing about Nietzsche or Weltanschauung?"

"That's all"

Before I leave for work the following morning, I call my psychiatrist, a man I parted company with many years ago, on very good terms—we sat looking at one another one day with no desire to say another word. The phone rings, a hollow ring in his space, and I place the receiver on the kitchen table, dash to the staircase. I listen for my wife upstairs. She's not the sneaky type but just might get it into her head to pick up the extension phone. Back to the phone, hear the trouble signal and dial again.

"What do you know, really know, about Kissinger?" I ask.

"Do you want an appointment?" the man says, "really need one?"

"No," I say, "not if you'll answer one question." A silence that extends. "Are you Jewish?"

"In our business, Hank, even the Christians are Jewish."

I ponder this question all day at work, and three times while I'm calculating the cost of erecting a new retail outlet in the Marietta Shopping Center, the computer signals START AGAIN, like TILT on the pinball machines. I can't wait to get home and start my hunt for Rudy. To find him, before Saturday, I must visit the gym every night. I scour the pool, locker room, universal gym room, wrestling room; stick my head into the steam room, can't see, whisper, Rudy, Rudy; someone hollers shut the door, try the paddle-ball court on the roof, and something new—the methol-lyptus room, a small box where naked men sit breathing in vapors like mentholated cough drops.

When Daisy catches me running off again on Thursday, carrying my little blue bag, she grabs my arm. "Wait, love. Did I ever tell you how Hitler helped the Egyptian women? A sergeant-major, snuffling into his moustache, told me at a wedding. Before Hitler, the men rode on their camels in the desert and the women walked behind."

"I've got to leave!"

"But afterwards, they started walking in front."

"Yeah—"

"They were looking for land mines."

I tear myself loose, but can I blame her when she shakes her head and says venomously, "Flaming youth." I warm up the car and duck back into the garage, and on our oversized appointments calendar posted next to the grocery shelves I write in large block print SEX ON FRIDAY.

At the swimming pool, I place my bag containing key, towel, and glasses on a folding chair. I see, leaning against the next chair, a flesh-colored thigh and leg standing in a Clark desert boot. A left boot. Same brand I favor. I look for the owner in the water. Only two men swimming between the red-buoyed lanes; it could be either one. I'm ashamed to put my glasses back on and stare. I guess it belongs to the crawl-stroker; as he turns near me, he leaves no churning wake. I start for the deep end of the pool when I feel a blast of cold hallway air. I've found him. Rudy stands just inside the door.

For the first time, I walk to meet him. He turns his face away but I catch a glimpse of the crushed left side below his eye, a cheekbone missing.

"Anybody ever talk to you around here, Hank?"

"Sometimes."

"Not to me. They talk funny to each other. Like—I had two heart attacks. Doctor said I should keep up the golf. I shot a 41. He shot a 36. He had a six handicap. I'd shoot them between the eyes!"

I understand him. I'd heard, my brother moved to Carefree, Arizona. Heavy smoker. He's dying of lung cancer.

A brawny blond man stands at the ladder below us. He pulls himself up the ladder. Then, swinging his arms, he hops on one leg toward his artifical limb. He fits his stump into the pink thigh, smiles at us graciously, "How are you guys?" and walks away stiffly. I wonder if his bathing suit drips down and fills the empty book. I shiver.

"Oh, it's a vunderful healthy place—this Y.M.C.A. of yours," Rudy says.

"Supreme arrogance, Rudy, vunderful, vunderful. You and Kissinger. You both hang on to that accent, vunderful. You must love it. There's a Polish emigré in my office; in just six years, he became a computer programmer and speaks perfect English." I start for the diving board, then turn back to him. "Is there anyone you like, Rudy? Besides Kissinger. And where in the hell did you come from?"

"Auschwitz."

"No! But where did you come from?"

"Auschwitz. I was born there."

It's as if I always knew. It had to be. That place. "Your people?"

"Mother—an inmate—Jewess probably. Maybe not. Father: who knows—another Jew? Then why was I kept alive? A *kapo,* a Jewish trusty, was the father, or a guard—if she was pretty enough—" His voice is emotionless, trails off, and he keeps his distance; always before, he nestled close to me, so close I couldn't breathe.

I stare. He's taking great deep gulps of air. "And you grew up there—how?"

His powerful chest heaves. His mouth opens, still no words,

closes. "I was only a child. A mouse ran across the sack over my legs. For three nights, I waited for the mouse to return. Then it too disappeared. What does a child know? Remember, it's all normal—if it's all he knows."

I know it is time to stop breathing. But one can only stop so long. Try it! Try not breathing. Kissinger: traitor—why didn't you die with them, why didn't you die with us!

Your insides float up to your throat. Everything bursts inside. You have to start breathing again.

Cry Uncle

"Dear Unc:

I am always wonderful these days. God's loving will compasses all beauty, so what need is there for anything but joy even in trial and hardship?

I didn't write this. The desire that sometimes arises is the selfish desire to record a beautiful prayer that should remain a silent communion between the lover and the beloved; and so it remains closer to purity by its silence. It was written.

God Is God Is God Is God Is God Is God Is God Is God Is God Is
Tai Tai Tai
Meher Baba
Beloved Darling, no other
is sought
And then nothing at all
shall ever be sought for anything.
Thy Will my shield and portions be
in whatever form I can ever see You in—
Starvation, elation, lust, torture
flattery, oppression,
diversion, and
bliss.
Always yours, in God's
ceaseless love.
Your numero two nephew
Ronnie

P.S. My girl friend, Jeanette, was discharged from the crazy house. She is unhappy."

That drivel from a young man descended from atheists. I pat my wallet pocket: the folded directions to Nassau General Hospital are in the compartment with my driver's license.

The kid was almost named after me but Jewish law wouldn't permit it. I knew he was in trouble, deep trouble, when I came home on army furlough and sat in my middle brother's overheated apartment, sweating. Ronnie's mother had this six-month-old boy dressed in wool, wearing booties and wrapped in a blanket. All you could see was a red, puckered, hot face.

I don't know what my atomic-energy brother did to him. Maurice, who is eleven years older than I, used to rap me on the arm when he got mad. I scattered the chess game he was playing with brother Bill once; he rapped me hard and I went after him. Holding me off with one hand, he tapped me on the arm and shoulder with the other and I counted aloud twenty-two, twenty-three, twenty-four taps or more, kept counting while I surged forward, tried to reach him because each tap had to be repaid in blood—equal tapping on his arm. The number of blows mounted and it seemed I'd never be able to pay him back.

I got to him years later. Maurice, Bill, my teacher-brother, and I drove to Valley Stream Park to play pick-up soccer. We played and rested, picnicked, drank beer, a good brother day, and after lunch, now a strong eighteen-year-old, I took them both on; tussled on the grass and pinned each one in turn after a sharp struggle. I liked my brothers from that day on.

I ball Ron's letter in my fist and loft it into the wastebasket ten feet away.

Armed with a wife and a couple of small daughters, I visited atomic-energy Maurice, his tiny wife and two sons. Ronnie's thirteenth birthday, so I bought him a catcher's mitt. I went searching for the boys in a nearby park and found them shooting baskets with two friends. Ron was wearing a stiff blue peajacket; the others had thrown sweaters and jackets aside and played in shirtsleeves. Watching them through the cyclone fence, I noticed that when Ron tried a layup, he was jumping off his left foot and shooting left-handed like me. All wrong. I walked over and waited at midcourt. Ron threw the ball toward me. I caught it, chucked a looping set shot that swished through the net and came down for a follow-up. My older nephew grabbed the ball out of Ron's hands and fed it, and I dribbled for an easy layup.

The four boys lined up and I flipped them bounce passes or gave hand-offs, and they heaved up their one-handers. No two-handed shooters anymore. The last two-handed artists I remember were the Jews and Blacks from City College beating Kentucky in the old Madison Square Garden. Maurice and I in the side balcony—couldn't see the players when the game flowed to our side. No need to talk as we found the rhythm; first they came racing down one side of the court and then circled the basketball stanchion and lined up on the opposite side. Still my left-handed nephew pushed off on the wrong foot. I demonstrated how to shoot left-handed and push off from the right foot. He tried, couldn't do it. The other boys watched skeptically. Ron, I said, hugging him to me, my right hand around his shoulder, take off that stiff coat—with freer movement you can shoot better. I started to unbutton his top button, and he pulled away, kicked the ball that was lying near the foul line, and ran off the court. I guess my mouth hung open because my older nephew said, it's not your fault, Uncle Dave. He never takes his coat off. He was just telling the guys what a good basketball player you were. Wasn't he guys, and he turned to the other two boys who nodded vigorously, and how you're the biggest uncle he's got. I should have spent more time with the kid. Taken him backpacking, canoeing, or—

Atomic-energy Maurice called a few weeks later. How are you? How are you? How are the kids? How are the kids? Fine. Fine. We're equal now: both with wife and children. Then we talked.

They're asking questions about you, Maurice said. My annual security clearance.

They never asked me before. What kind of questions?

About the camp you're treasurer of. What sort of camp is it? Are there communists on the Board? Any communist children as campers? An agent wants to interview you in New York. At your convenience.

No.

What should I tell them?

Tell them it's an interracial camp.

They won't be satisfied. My job—

That's all you tell them.

Can't you come in? They promised it would only take an hour or less—to help me out—

No! Not a chance.

He hung up.

The following day he phoned again. After a rerun I told him, just say you never see me, never visited, tell them we're estranged, that you only see me at funerals and weddings and bar mitzvahs. I don't remember what he said but I hung up. I saw him three times in the next six years. Always at funerals, and the last time we walked side by side, struggling under the same end of a coffin. He grew ashen-faced, waiting at the funeral parlor's rear entrance, waiting for the usual wheeled cart on which we expected to trundle the corpse to the hearse, but the cart never came. A long walk. Together.

After Ron dropped out of Stony Brook, he wrote to me (didn't think it was anything to worry about, dropping out was quite the vogue then).

"Dear Uncle Dave:

I've had jobs as a dish stacker, cashier, waiter, typist, and in each job I made my usual unbelievably stupid errors. I tried to go back to Stony Brook but after an hour there with the same nauseating people and disgusting architecture—I gave up.

The cleavage of my mind*********_____*_____******
------- + + + + +19+ + + + +----__ + + +
*****19----********19------
----***** _____ -------*****

I never used the catcher's mitt you bought me but I still have it.

Your nephew,

Ron."

Ronnie's next six years: Mt. Sinai Hospital, Hillside, Creedmoor.

other places. He'd start out on the subway, panic, call my brother, and end up where he felt safe, in a hospital. In and out the rotating doors and always letters.

"Dear Unc:

I'm working in the Fountain House Thrift Shop. Picked up furniture from Mrs. Basil Rathbone, a nice old witch, remember her husband played Sherlock Holmes in those '40s films. She gave us sherry. At the After Care Clinic, the dentist drilled my wisdom tooth but it didn't help much.

Girls are goddesses, baseball players are heros, and weather reports are dramatic. I know that's not normal thinking, Unc. I have a new psychiatrist: a kid said he's called Leave-'Em-In-Lebovic. If I say a wrong word—they'll put me back in Creedmoor."

I usually answered the letters but only visited once. A cavernous reception room, vaulted ceiling like a railway station, all gray-speckled travertine floor. Inside, in another large room with scattered metal chairs and a settee in front of a television set, I found Ron wearing a dirty bathrobe and slippers. How does this nuthouse compare to the others? I asked him. The worst, he said. See that black guy with the mop? He's an attendant. Called a psychiatric aide. He gets worked up sometimes and throws the mop handle from one end of the room to the other, yelling Mau-Mau, Kenya! Ron shivered. He's worse than the nuts inside. I slipped him a few dollars. He returned the money with, don't need it here. They'll mug and roll you if they know you have money.

The staff went on strike a few weeks later and all the patients were sent home. When the strike was over, many of them did not return. Did their parents want them outside?

I tried to imagine his life at home doing nothing. Bereft of our family's Jewish-Puritan work ethic. Watches TV until 4:00 A.M. Sleeps past noon. Listens to Buddy Holly records. Leaves the house only to replenish the grocery stock with money his father left. Takes thorazine. Buys more books on philosophy and psychology. But I saw a stack of them on my only visit to Creedmoor: some books in original mailing wrappers; others, the pages were uncut. Mother dead, another funeral. I saw Ron. He didn't cry. Father spends most of his time at his lady friend's house in Port Jefferson. My brother is the only guy I can imagine with a lady friend. Other men have a woman, a fiancée, a bedmate, a trick, a chick or a cunt, a what-not, but a lady friend, only Maurice. Ron stopped writing and I couldn't call Maurice—except if we're lucky enough to have another funeral in the family.

Finally—"Unc, I'm so ashamed. I made an utter fool of myself. I bought four teen-age magazines: *TV Radio Talk, Fave, Sixteen,* and *Flip.* Why? What do they all have in common? Well, besides being written for half-witted teen-age girls, they all contain pictures of Peggy Lipton, the female lead in TV's Mod Squad. BUT I'M WORKING!!!!!

A real job, not a made-up one in an After Care Center. In a card and book shop. Unc, I can use a few bucks until I get my first pay-check. An old Jewish grandma returned a card because it had two black hands clasped. Then a young black woman came in pushing a baby carriage and asks do you have any Black cards? I knew what she meant but I couldn't answer. So I walked over to the section of the store that has dog-to-dog cards and my-cat-to-your-cat cards (they hired me to sell books, not this shit), and pointed to a box which had a little black girl in pigtails on the display cutout. Is that what you mean, I said? Now wasn't that dumb. I quit after that. But I stuck it out three weeks. You're mad now, Unc, admit it."

I called on someone who owed me a favor, never did this before, and got Ron a job as a telephone solicitor working for C.C.I. on Fifty-fourth and Lexington Avenue. They employed 146 telephone solicitors.

Now Ron started to call me every single night. He sounded better and better, best I've ever heard him sound. I'd just say, well, what happened today, Ron?

"I'm moving along, Unc. They started me on *Skeptic Magazine,* reminding junior high school teachers that their sub ran out. A polite class of people. Then, I was advanced to Dur-Drill, can drill your own well by rigging the drill to a Ford pickup, and with a few extra attachments on the easy-payment plan, you can drill for oil. All the magazine responses are from down South, that's where I phone."

Another night: "I tried to sell a Bull-Worker exerciser in Boston. Fellow answered, what's your name. Davidson, I said. I don't know why I picked that name—just leaped out at me. Look here, Davidson, he yelled, you woke me up and woke my whole family up, and wokened up the dog, and he's barking and I'm coming to New York, gonna look up all the Davidsons in the phone book, and I'm going to find you and beat the shit out of you."

I started looking forward to Ron's calls.

"I've been promoted, Unc. They skipped me right past *Saturday Review* and I'm on the big time, selling *TV Guide*, their hottest property. Polite down in Plains, Georgia, they hear your entire spiel. Now I don't really want to renew, it's not your fault, you sound like a right nice fella, but the magazine came all battered and chewed up, probably the postmaster's dog and all that but no, I don't want any more magazines.

Unc, listen to what a fellow said from Gatlinburg. Said I sounded like a right nice fella and if I ever came down that way, I should be sure to look him up. Get a pencil now, fella, he said, just write down these directions.

Unc, Unc—I like these people on the other end. They're the nicest people I ever met. Even the little old ladies in Illinois, that's the toughest state, and one of them answered today, I don't want it, not for fifty-two weeks, not for two weeks, not if it's free. Bang went her receiver."

Then the phone calls that came regularly at 8:00 P.M. stopped.

A couple of weeks went by and my atomic-energy brother phoned. Another funeral? Without even a hello, how are you, he started in. "Why! Why! I don't understand it. Ronnie climbed to no. 46 in the standings. He scored a perfect seven last week from the monitor who listens to their calls. A SEVEN, perfect for persuasion, diction, temperament, patience, and three more things. David! I found him wandering in the subway. He said, ants are invading the house. Ants! He said, my teeth are falling apart. I've got to take him in. I can't do it alone. I can't call the cops. His doctor told me he might—"

I cut my brother short. "I'm leaving work now. I'll grab a cab."

I sat in the back with Ron, who's huddled in an overcoat—a warm spring day—and staring at his knuckles. My brother reached into his inside breast pocket and handed back the directions. I knew he wanted me to read them aloud. I read: "Southern State to Meadowbrook Parkway, exit 25 or 26 (too loud, lowered my voice), first one is north, right turn onto Hempstead Turnpike, continue east and then watch for a high building on the left. This is Nassau General Hospital. Just before the hospital, make a left turn at a big shopping center, into the visitors' parking lot. Go around to the old building. Maurice," I said, "why did you pick me to go along today?"

"You think I wanted to go way out here? Mt. Sinai doesn't have room. The doctor said I shouldn't take Ronnie alone in a cab. He's nervous about changing hospitals."

"Our oldest brother?"

"No good. I remember he couldn't make up his mind if he wanted an ice cream cone."

I opened my shirt collar and started to slip out of my suit jacket. Ron twisted left and reached for the car-door latch. Jacket hanging from my right shoulder, I grabbed his wrist and pushed him back into the seat. I locked his right arm with mine, felt like a prison warden. He slumped back, turned up his coat collar, shrinking into it so only the top of his head and forehead were visible.

When we pulled into the parking lot, Maurice flipped the keys at me. "I can handle it now," he said. "I know you want to get back to work. Just leave the car at my garage—the Shell station at the corner. You can get back to the City in thirty minutes by cab. Thanks."

And then, three months later, I'm back on the same parkways, the crumpled directions lying on the seat beside me. The sun is an orange flame in the west. When I started the drive, the steering wheel was so hot I drove with my fingertips. A ten-foot-high cyclone fence surrounds the parking lot.

I get a pass. Clutching it, swing to the right. Flash pass and an unarmed guard waves me on. Walk past a bank of elevators. Stop at a desk, wave me on; I'm circling, circling the entire lobby floor; show my pass, on—on—a guard points to a single elevator. Ride up. Walk along a green corridor. I pass two uniformed men lounging in a small room. They wear strapped-down pistols in black holsters. One man walks out and I show my pass. He opens a closed door with a thick wire glass window across the top. I walk on, short way, another green corridor, and stop before another locked door. Clock above door. Time 6:45. I look through six-by-eight-inch glass opening; can't find Ronnie. Bathrobed figures walk up and back inside. Some wear pants and shirts. They walk in slow aimless patterns. They wash up to the door and, ignoring it, walk back down their enclave.

I eavesdrop on a black mother and white mother who are praising their sons. One was a brilliant mathematician; the other a shining poet. A black face presses nose against the other side of the glass. The mother curls her fingers in greeting. The face disappears. A quiet crowd is gathering behind me. At exactly 7:00 P.M., the door is opened. I defer to the two mothers at the threshold. The black mother slips ahead. The other woman hesitates, then follows. We all file in.

Many doors open onto a long brown-tiled corridor. The same apple-green walls. All the doors have peephole windows, six by eight inches. Two doors on the right-hand side are shut. I wander down the corridor. Visitors hug inmates. Into the small dayroom at the end of the hall. The two green plastic-covered couches and all the chrome-legged chairs are taken. Out again. I backtrack, looking for Ron.

He comes shambling out of a door on the right-hand side. He needs a haircut. His suntans are dirty, like he pissed in them. Shirt wrinkled and hanging out of pants. He tucks his shirt front into pants. Pants are too short, no socks, and the black shoes are laced through only the top eyehole.

I shake his hand, hold it for a moment. He turns away and I follow him into his room. Two beds, gray army blankets over them, walls are housing-project tan, one chest piled with clothes, six nails hammered into an unpainted two-by-four over the chest, one chair. He lies down on the right-hand bed and motions me to the other. I slide in sideways, and sit facing him.

He speaks: "You cause me to bear up even under my own inability
    to be Your Own True Lover

Your True Slave, Your Tone Dust"

He closes his eyes: "I am paralyzed and babbling in thanking and loving you

and subjugating myself to you as Ali

for Everything

And for what Exists

beyond Everything"

One eye opens and shuts again: "Thank you God, Thank you for you as You

and Thank you for you as Baba

That all else will be manifestly you

as BABA is

Halle! Halle! Hallelujah!"

I wince, squeeze the knuckles of my left hand with my right. Squeeze harder.

"Knew you'd hate that shit," he says. "But you came."

"I'm here, Ron."

"Hey Unc, tell Dad not to touch my books."

"How many have you got?" I remember his bedroom overflowing with them. Three six-foot shelves, books in cartons, under the bed, everywhere.

"He might try and sell them. Promise me. You've got influence. He won't fuck around with you."

I nod.

"Hey Unc, you remember the time we were coming home from a wedding in a cab?" He sits up, clasps his hands in back of his head. "Me, Dad, Mom, and Grandpa." (His brother too but he left him out.) "Grandpa said the driver gave us a bumpy ride, and he picked up a garbage can and raised it over his head. That driver was afraid to get out of the cab."

I remember parking behind them and bolting out the door. Maurice and I wrestled the can away from my father (how the hell did he lift it with his white muscle-less arms?) and I gave the cabbie a big tip to shove off.

"He was a tough nut, Grandpa."

"You need anything? A couple of books, some clean clothes?"

Why didn't I bring a gift, anything.

"No, I don't read anymore. I'm twenty-seven years old. I had a girl once. Met her at Creedmoor. After the strike, we didn't go back. She was nuts! I sat around eating chocolate cake. Always kept a spare chocolate cake in the freezer and one in the bread drawer. She was as nutty as I am."

A thin young girl wanders in. She wears a clean white blouse, a slash of ruby lipstick across her mouth. "My boyfriend didn't come," she says.

Ron swings his legs to the floor. "Sit down next to me, Flossie." He pats the blanket. "Visiting hours aren't over yet. He may still come along." She sits very carefully, but when her bottom touches the bed, she springs up as if it were a hot griddle and runs out of the room.

Hammering sounds from across the hall. I can see the locked door shiver. "Bastards! Let me out of here. Scumbags! Let me out. Lincoln freed the slaves. FREE ME! FREE ME!

"Why don't they do something?" I say.

"He's not the worst. He wears pants. Watch out for the bathrobe guys. He already got a needle this afternoon. He'll stop soon."

Dark shadows now near the doorway; a long silence until the sun moves across the blankets.

"I prop the chair against the knob at night," Ron says, "and jam the chest against the chair."

Visiting hours are over. I hear echoing down the hall. The head of Ron's bed is licked by a rapidly disappearing orange glow.

"When are you coming out, Ron?"

"Later, don't I always come out? I'm at the head of the class here. We'll be moving into a new wing soon. Get away from the head-bangers. I saw the new suites on a field trip, not at all bad. Training for the outside and all that."

The corridor holds its breath, lies still. No feet parading by. The banging starts again, loud and fierce—voiceless, then drops off and expires.

"When the shades of night fall over Nutville, Unc, it gets pretty grim in here."

I stand up. Right foot's asleep. Stamp and wiggle my toes. Bad circulation. Bad blood. I take a few sliding steps to get out from between the beds.

Ron calls, "Hey Unc. Bring me a light bulb if you come again."

I nod.

"When the lights go out, they tell me, it takes three to four days to get another bulb. How long does one bulb last? Better bring a couple of bulbs." He duckwalks along the bed and sits at the foot.

I touch his shoulder, turn to go, and wonder—why, why can't I love him more?